Tonight.

The decision came to her as effortlessly as it had the first time. Tonight they would be together, and if it was only once—if once was all he wanted—it would be enough.

Sitting in the crowded stadium, Asher felt the thrill of desire as clearly as though she had been naked in Ty's arms. She felt no shame; it was natural. She felt no fear; it was inevitable. Years made up of long, unending days vanished.

What a waste of time, she thought suddenly. No, a loss, she corrected herself. A loss of time—nothing's ever wasted. *Tonight.* The long wait was over, and she laughed aloud in relief and joy.

NORA ROBERTS
lives with her two sons in the Blue Ridge Mountains of western Maryland. To be a published author was her lifetime dream, which she has seen fulfilled in the many books she has written for Silhouette. Renowned for her warm characters and wit, Nora Roberts is a favorite with readers of romance.

Dear Reader:

Romance readers have been enthusiastic about Silhouette Special Editions for years. And that's not by accident: Special Editions were the first of their kind and continue to feature realistic stories with heightened romantic tension.

The longer stories, sophisticated style, greater sensual detail and variety that made Special Editions popular are the same elements that will make you want to read book after book.

We hope that you enjoy this Special Edition today, and will enjoy many more.

The Editors at Silhouette Books

NORA ROBERTS
Opposites Attract

Silhouette Special Edition
Published by Silhouette Books New York

America's Publisher of Contemporary Romance

SILHOUETTE BOOKS, a Division of Simon & Schuster, Inc.
1230 Avenue of the Americas, New York, N.Y. 10020

Distributed by Pocket Books

ISBN: 0-671-53699-0

First Silhouette Books printing November, 1984

10 9 8 7 6 5 4 3 2 1

America's Publisher of Contemporary Romance

Printed in the U.S.A.

BC91

Books by Nora Roberts

Silhouette Romance

Irish Thoroughbred #81
Blithe Images #127
Song of the West #143
Search for Love #163
Island of Flowers #180
From This Day #199
Her Mother's Keeper #215
Untamed #252
Storm Warning #274
Sullivan's Woman #280
Less of a Stranger #299

Silhouette Special Edition

The Heart's Victory #59
Reflections #100
Dance of Dreams #116
First Impressions #162
The Law Is a Lady #175
Opposites Attract #199

Silhouette Intimate Moments

Once More with Feeling #2
Tonight and Always #12
This Magic Moment #25
Endings and Beginnings #33
A Matter of Choice #49
Rules of the Game #70

Pocket Books

Promise Me Tomorrow

For Joan Schulhafer,
leader of tours, handler of details and good friend

Opposites Attract

GLOSSARY

ACE—A served ball that is not successfully returned by the receiver.

ADVANTAGE—The next point won after a score of "deuce".

BASE LINE—The back line at either end of the court.

CENTER SERVICE COURT—The line dividing the service court into right and left service courts.

DEUCE—The score called when both players have won three points. Two successive points after deuce by one player are necessary to win.

DOUBLE FAULT—Two service faults in succession.

FAULT—A served ball that does not land in the proper court or is not served properly.

GAME—Unit of scoring next higher than the point. Scored when one side has won four points.

IN PLAY—The ball is considered in play from the time it is served until the point has been made.

LET or LET BALL—A served ball that touches the net but lands in the proper court. The service may be replayed and is not a fault.

LOB—A high arched shot over the net.

LOVE—The equivalent of zero or no points in scoring.

POINT—The smallest unit of scoring. The first point is called 15, the second point 30, and the third point 40. The fourth point is game.

RALLY—The exchange of the ball over the net; ends when one player fails to make the return.

RECEIVER—The player who receives the serve.

SERVE—To put the ball in play.

SERVICE COURTS—The two center sections of a court, bisected by the net, within which a served ball must land.

SERVICE LINE—The line across the back of the service courts, parallel with the net.

SET—The unit of scoring next higher than a game, usually consisting of six games first won by 1 player. Margin over opponent must be at least 2 games; if not, play is continued until 2-game lead is obtained, ending the set.

SMASH—A hard, swift, overhand stroke.

VOLLEY—To hit the ball before it touches the ground (except in serving).

Chapter One

"Advantage, Starbuck."

Isn't it always? Asher mused. For a moment the large arena held that humming silence peculiar to indoor sports events. There was an aroma of roasted peanuts and sweat. The overhead lights heated the scent somewhat pleasantly while the crush of bodies added enforced camaraderie. A small child sent up a babbling complaint and was hushed.

Seated several rows back at mid-court, Asher Wolfe watched Ty Starbuck—tennis master, Gypsy, eternal boy of summer and former lover. She thought again, as she had several times during more than two hours of play, that he'd changed. Just how wasn't yet completely clear. More than three years had passed since she'd seen him in the flesh. But he hadn't aged, or thickened, or lost any of his characteristic verve.

Rarely over the years had she watched a televised match—it was too painful. Too many faces were familiar, with his the most strictly avoided. If Asher had chanced to come across a write-up or picture of him in the sports pages or in a gossip column, she had immediately put it aside. Ty Starbuck was out of her life. Her decision. Asher was a very decisive woman.

Even her decision to come to the U.S. Indoor Tennis Championship had been a cool-headed one. Before making the trip, she had carefully weighed the pros and cons. In the end logic had won. She was getting back into the game herself. On the circuit, meetings with Ty would be unavoidable. She would see him now, letting the press, her colleagues and fans see clearly that there was nothing left of what had been three years before. Ty would see too, and, she hoped fervently, so would she.

Ty stood behind the baseline, preparing to serve. His stance was the same, she mused, as was his sizzling concentration. He tossed the ball up, coming back and over with the wicked left-handed serve that had become synonymous with his name, a Starbuck.

Asher heard the explosion of his breath that forced the power into it. She held her own. A lesser player than the Frenchman, Grimalier, would never have gotten a racket on the ball. His return was quick—force meeting force—and the rally began.

The crowd grew noisier as the ball smashed and thudded. Echoes bounced crazily. There were cries of encouragement, shouts of appreciation for the prowess of the two players. Ty's basic entertainment value hadn't decreased since Asher had been out of the game. Fans adored or detested him, but they never, never ignored him. Nor could she, though she was no longer certain which category she fell into. Every muscle of his body was familiar to her, every move, every expression. Her feelings were a confused jumble of respect, admiration and longing, which swirled to reach a vortex of pain, sharply remembered. Still, she was caught up in him again. Ty Starbuck demanded every last emotion and didn't really give a damn if it was love or hate.

Both men moved quickly, their eyes riveted on the small white sphere. Backhand, forehand, drop shot. Sweat poured down unheeded. Both the game and the fans demanded it. A tennis buff wanted to see the effort, the strain, wanted to hear the grunts and whistling breaths, wanted to smell the sweat. Despite her determination to remain dispassionate, Asher found herself watching Ty with the undiluted admiration she'd held for him for more than ten years.

He played with nonchalant flash—contradictory terms, but there it was. Strength, agility, form—he had them all. He had a long, limber body, seemingly elastic until the muscles flowed and bunched. His six-two height gave him an advantage of reach, and he could twist and turn on a dime. He played like a fencer—Asher had always thought a swashbuckler. Graceful sweeps, lunges, parries, with an almost demonic glint in his dusk-gray eyes. His face was that of the adventurer—narrow, rakish, with a hint of strong bone vying with an oddly tender mouth. As always, his hair was a bit too long, flowing wild and black around a white sweatband.

He was a set-up, and held advantage, but he played as though his life depended on this one point. That hadn't changed, Asher thought, as her heart pounded at double time. She was as involved in the match as if she were the one with the racket in her hand and the sweat rolling over her skin. Her palms were slick, her own muscles tight. Tennis involved its onlookers. Starbuck absorbed them. That hadn't changed either.

Ty smashed the ball crosscourt at the sideline. It careened away even as the Frenchman dove toward it. Asher sucked in her breath at the speed and placement of the ball.

"Wide," the line judge said dispassionately. A loud complaint poured out of the crowd. Asher fixed her eyes on Ty and waited for the explosion.

He stood, breathing hard from the punishing rally, his eyes fixed on the judge. The crowd continued to roar disapproval as deuce was called. Slowly, his eyes still on the judge, Ty swiped his wristband over his brow. His face was inscrutable but for his eyes, and his eyes spoke volumes. The crowd quieted to a murmur of speculation. Asher bit hard on her bottom lip. Ty walked back to the baseline without having uttered a sound.

This was the change, Asher realized with a jolt. Control. Her breath came out slowly as the tension in her shoulders diminished. In years past, Ty Starbuck would have hurled abuse—and an occasional racket—snarled, implored the crowd for support or berated them. Now he walked silently across the service court with temper smoldering in his eyes. But he held it in check. This was something new.

Behind the baseline Ty took his time, took his stance, then cracked an ace, like a bullet from a gun. The crowd screamed for him. With a quiet, insolent patience he waited while the scoring was announced. Again, he held advantage. Knowing him, and others like him, Asher was aware that his mind was occupied with his next move. The ace was already a memory, to be taken out and savored later. He still had a game to win.

The Frenchman connected with the next serve with a blazing forehand smash. The volley was sweating, furious and blatantly male. It was all speed and fire, two pirates blasting at each other across a sea of hardwood. There was the sound of the ball hitting the heart of the racket, the skid of rubber soles on wood, the grunts of the competitors as they drew out more force, all drowned beneath the echoes of cheers. The crowd was on its feet. Asher was on hers without even being aware of it. Neither man gave quarter as the seconds jumped to a minute, and a minute to more.

With a swing of the wrist the Frenchman returned a nearly impossible lob that drove him behind the baseline. The ball landed deep in the right court. With a forceful backhand Ty sent the ball low and away from his opponent, ending the two-and-a-half-hour match, three sets to one.

Starbuck was the U.S. Indoor Tennis champion, and the crowd's hero.

Asher let the enthusiasm pour around her as Ty walked to the net for the traditional handshake. The match had affected her more than she'd anticipated, but she passed this off as professional admiration.

Now she allowed herself to wonder what his reaction would be when he saw her again.

Had she hurt him? His heart? His pride? The pride, she mused. That she could believe. The heart was a different matter. He would be angry, she concluded. She would be cool. Asher knew how to maintain a cool exterior as well as she knew how to smash an overhead lob. She'd learned it all as a child. When they met, she would simply deploy his temper. She had been preparing for the first encounter almost as religiously as she had been preparing to pick up her profession again. Asher was going to win at both. After he had finished with the showers and the press, she would make it a point to seek him out. To congratulate him—and to present the next test. It was much wiser for her to make the first move, for her to be the one prepared. Confident, she watched Ty exchange words with Grimalier at the net.

Then Ty turned his head very slowly, very deliberately. With no searching through the crowd, no hesitation, his eyes locked on hers. The strength of the contact had her drawing in a sharp, unwilling breath. His eyes held, no wavering. Her mouth went dry. Then he smiled, an unpleasant, direct challenge. Asher met it, more from shock than temerity as the crowd bellowed his name. *Starbuck* echoed from the walls like a litany. Ten seconds—fifteen— he neither blinked nor moved. For a man of action he had an uncanny ability for stillness. Boring into hers, his eyes made the distance between them vanish. The smile remained fixed. Just as Asher's palms began to sweat, he turned a full circle for the crowd, his racket above his head like a lance. They adored him.

He'd known, Asher thought furiously as people swarmed around her. He had known all along that she was there. Her anger wasn't the hot, logical result of being outmaneuvered, but small, silver slices of cold fury. Ty had let her know in ten seconds, without words, that the game was still on. And he always won.

Not this time though, she told herself. She had changed too. But she stood where she was, rooted, staring out at the now empty court. Her thoughts were whirling with memories, emotions, remembered sensations. People brushed by her, already debating the match.

She was a tall, reed-slim figure tanned gold from hours in the sun. Her hair was short, sculptured and misty-blond. The style flattered, while remaining practical for her profession. Over three years of retirement, Asher hadn't altered it. Her face seemed more suited to the glossy pages of a fashion magazine than the heat and frenzy of a tennis court. A weekender, one might think, looking at her elegant cheekbones in an oval face. Not a pro. The nose was small and straight above a delicately molded mouth she rarely thought to tint. Makeup on the courts was a waste of time, as sweat would wash it away. Her eyes were large and round, a shade of blue that hinted at violet. One of her few concessions to vanity was to darken the thick pale lashes that surrounded them. While other women competitors added jewelry or ribbons and bows to the court dress, Asher had never thought of it. Even off the court her attire leaned toward the simple and muted.

An enterprising reporter had dubbed her "The Face" when she had been nineteen. She'd been nearly twenty-three when she had retired from professional play, but the name had stuck. Hers was a face of great beauty and rigid control. On court, not a flicker of expression gave her opponent or the crowd a hint of what she was thinking or feeling. One of her greatest defenses in the game was her ability to remain unruffled under stress. The standard seeped into her personal life.

Asher had lived and breathed tennis for so long that the line of demarcation between woman and athlete was smudged. The hard, unbendable rule, imposed by her father, was ingrained into her—privacy, first and last. Only one person had ever been able to cross the boundary. Asher was determined he would not do so again.

As she stood staring down at the empty court, her face told nothing of her anger or turmoil—or the pain she hadn't been prepared for. It was calm and aloof. Her concentration was so deep that the leader of the small packet of people that approached her had to speak her name twice to get her attention.

She'd been recognized, she discovered. Though Asher had known it was inevitable, it still gave her a twist of pleasure to sign the papers and programs thrust at her. She hadn't been forgotten.

The questions were easy to parry, even when they skirted close to her relationship with Ty. A smile and double-talk worked well with fans. Asher wasn't naïve enough to think it would work with reporters. That, she hoped, was for another day.

As she signed, and edged her way back, Asher spotted a few colleagues—an old foe, a former doubles partner, a smattering of faces from the past. Her eyes met Chuck Prince's. Ty's closest friend was an affable player with a wrist of steel and beautiful footwork. Though the silent exchange was brief, even friendly, Asher saw the question in his eyes before she gave her attention to the next fan.

The word's out, she thought almost grimly as she smiled at a teenage tennis buff. Asher Wolfe's picking up her racket again. And they'd wonder, and eventually ask, if she was picking up Ty Starbuck too.

"Asher!" Chuck moved to her with the same bouncy stride he used to cross a court. In his typical outgoing style he seized her by the shoulders and kissed her full on the mouth. "Hey, you look terrific!"

With a laugh Asher drew back the breath his greeting had stolen from her. "So do you." It was inevitably true. Chuck was average in almost every way—height, build, coloring. But his inner spark added appeal and a puckish sort of sexuality. He'd never hesitated to exploit it—good-naturedly.

"No one knew you were coming," Chuck complained, easing her gently through the thinning crowd. "I didn't know you were here until . . ." His voice trailed off so that Asher knew he referred to the ten seconds of potent contact with Ty. "Until after the match," he finished. He gave her shoulder a quick squeeze. "Why didn't you give someone a call?"

"I wasn't entirely sure I'd make it." Asher allowed herself to be negotiated to a clear spot in a rear hallway. "Then I thought I'd just melt into the crowd. It didn't seem fair to disrupt the match with any the-prodigal-returns business."

"It was a hell of a match." The flash of teeth gleamed with enthusiasm. "I don't know if I've ever seen Ty play better than he did in the last set. Three aces."

"He always had a deadly serve," Asher murmured.

"Have you seen him?"

From anyone else the blunt question would have earned a cold stare. Chuck earned a quick grimace. "No. I will, of course, but I didn't want to distract him before the match." Asher linked her fingers—an old nervous habit. "I didn't realize he knew I was here."

Distract Starbuck, she thought with an inner laugh. No one and nothing distracted him once he picked up his game racket.

"He went crazy when you left."

Chuck's quiet statement brought her back. Deliberately she unlaced her fingers. "I'm sure he recovered quickly." Because the retort was sharper than she had intended, Asher shook her head as if to take back the words. "How have you been? I saw an ad with you touting the virtues of a new line of tennis shoes."

"How'd I look?"

"Sincere," she told him with a quick grin. "I nearly went out and bought a pair."

He sighed. "I was shooting for macho."

As the tension seeped out of her, Asher laughed. "With that face?" She cupped his chin with her hand and moved it from side to side. "It's a face a mother could trust—foolishly," she added.

"Shh!" He glanced around in mock alarm. "Not so loud, my reputation."

"Your reputation suffered a few dents in Sydney," she recalled. "What was that—three seasons ago? The stripper."

"Exotic dancer," Chuck corrected righteously. "It was merely an exchange of cultures."

"You did look kind of cute wearing those feathers." With another laugh she kissed his cheek. "Fuchsia becomes you."

"We all missed you, Asher." He patted her slim, strong shoulder.

The humor fled from her eyes. "Oh, Chuck, I missed you. Everyone, all of it. I don't think I realized just how much until I walked in here today." Asher looked into space at her own thoughts, her own memories. "Three years," she said softly.

"Now you're back."

Her eyes drifted to his. "Now I'm back," she agreed. "Or will be in two weeks."

"The Foro Italico."

Asher gave him a brief smile that was more determination than joy. "I've never won on that damn Italian clay. I'm going to this time."

"It was your pacing."

The voice from behind her had Asher's shoulders stiffening. As she faced Chuck her eyes showed only the merest flicker of some secret emotion before they calmed. When she turned to Ty he saw first that his memory of her beauty hadn't been exaggerated with time, and second that her layer of control was as tough as ever.

"So you always told me," she said calmly. The jolt was over, she reasoned, with the shock of eye contact in the auditorium. But her stomach muscles tightened. "You played beautifully, Ty . . . after the first set."

They were no more than a foot apart now. Neither could find any changes in the other. Three years, it seemed, was barely any time at all. It occurred to Asher abruptly that twenty years wouldn't have mattered. Her heart would still thud, her blood would still swim. For him. It had always, would always be for him. Quickly she pushed those thoughts aside. If she were to remain calm under his gaze, she couldn't afford to remember.

The press were still tossing questions at him, and now at her as well. They began to crowd in, nudging Asher closer to Ty. Without a word he took her arm and drew her through the door at his side. That it happened to be a woman's rest room didn't faze him as he turned the lock. He faced her, leaning lazily back against the door while Asher stood straight and tense.

As he had thirty minutes before, Ty took his time studying her. His eyes weren't calm, they rarely were, but the emotion in them was impossible to decipher. Even in his relaxed stance there was a sense of force, a storm brewing. Asher met his gaze levelly, as he expected. And she moved him. Her power of serenity always moved him. He could have strangled her for it.

"You haven't changed, Asher."

"You're wrong." Why could she no longer breathe easily or control the furious pace of her heart?

"Am I?" His brows disappeared under his tousled hair for a moment. "We'll see."

He was a very physical man. When he spoke, he gestured. When he held a conversation, he touched. Asher could remember the brush of his hand—on her arm, her hair, her shoulder. It had been his casualness that had drawn her to him. And had driven her away. Now, as they stood close, she was surprised that Ty did not touch her in any way. He simply watched and studied her.

"I noticed a change," she countered. "You didn't argue with the referees or shout at the line judge. Not once." Her lips curved slightly. "Not even after a bad call."

He gave her a lightly quizzical smile. "I turned over that leaf some time ago."

"Really?" She was uncomfortable now, but merely moved her shoulders. "I haven't been keeping up."

"Total amputation, Asher?" he asked softly.

"Yes." She would have turned away, but there was nowhere to go. Over the line of sinks to her left the mirrors tossed back her reflection . . . and his. Deliberately she shifted so that her back was to them. "Yes," she repeated, "it's the cleanest way."

"And now?"

"I'm going to play again," Asher responded simply. His scent was reaching out for her, that familiar, somehow heady fragrance that was sweat and victory and sex all tangled together. Beneath the placid expression her thoughts shot off in a tangent.

Nights, afternoons, rainy mornings. He'd shown her everything a man and woman could be together, opened doors she had never realized existed. He had knocked down every guard until he had found her.

Oh God, dear God, she thought frantically. Don't let him touch me now. Asher linked her fingers together. Though his eyes never left hers, Ty noted the gesture. And recognized it. He smiled.

"In Rome?"

Asher controlled the urge to swallow. "In Rome," she agreed. "To start. I'll go in unseeded. It has been three years."

"How's your backhand?"

"Good." Automatically she lifted her chin. "Better than ever."

Very deliberately Ty circled her arm with his fingers. Asher's palms became damp. "It was always a surprise," he commented, "the power in that slender arm. Still lifting weights?"

"Yes."

His fingers slid down until they circled the inside of her elbow. It gave him bitter pleasure to feel the tiny pulse jump erratically. "So," he murmured softly, "Lady Wickerton graces the courts again."

"Ms. Wolfe," Asher corrected him stiffly. "I've taken my maiden name back."

His glance touched on her ringless hands. "The divorce is final?"

"Quite final. Three months ago."

"Pity." His eyes had darkened with anger when he lifted them back to hers. "A title suits you so well. I imagine you fit into an English manor as easily as a piece of Wedgwood. Drawing rooms and butlers," he murmured, then scanned her face as if he would memorize it all over again. "You have the looks for them."

"The reporters are waiting for you." Asher made a move to her left in an attempt to brush by him. Ty's fingers clamped down.

"Why, Asher?" He'd promised himself if he ever saw her again, he wouldn't ask. It was a matter of pride. But pride was overwhelmed by temper as the question whipped out, stinging them both. "Why did you leave that way? Why did you run off and marry that damn English jerk without a word to me?"

She didn't wince at the pressure of his fingers, nor did she make any attempt to pull away. "That's my business."

"*Your* business?" The words were hardly out of her mouth before he grabbed both her arms. "*Your* business? We'd been together for months, the whole damn circuit that year. One night you're in my bed, and the next thing I know you've run off with some English lord." His control slipped another notch as he shook her. "I had to find out from my sister. You didn't even have the decency to dump me in person."

"Decency?" she tossed back. "I won't discuss

decency with you, Ty." She swallowed the words, the accusations she'd promised herself never to utter. "I made my choice," she said levelly, "I don't have to justify it to you."

"We were lovers," he reminded her tightly. "We lived together for nearly six months."

"I wasn't the first woman in your bed."

"You knew that right from the start."

"Yes, I knew." She fought the urge to beat at him with the hopeless rage that was building inside her. "I made my choice then, just as I made one later. Now, let me go."

Her cool, cultured control had always fascinated and infuriated him. Ty knew her, better than anyone, even her own father—certainly better than her ex-husband. Inside, she was jelly, shuddering convulsively, but outwardly she was composed and lightly disdainful. Ty wanted to shake her until she rattled. More, much more, he wanted to taste her again—obliterate three years with one long greedy kiss. Desire and fury hammered at him. He knew that if he gave in to either, he'd never be able to stop. The wound was still raw.

"We're not finished, Asher." But his grip relaxed. "You still owe me."

"No." Defensive, outraged, she jerked free. "No, I don't owe you anything."

"Three years," he answered, and smiled. The smile was the same biting challenge as before. "You owe me three years, and by God, you're going to pay."

He unlocked the door and opened it, stepping

back so that Asher had no choice but to meet the huddle of reporters head-on.

"Asher, how does it feel to be back in the States?"

"It's good to be home."

"What about the rumors that you're going to play professionally again?"

"I intend to play professionally beginning with the opening of the European circuit in Rome."

More questions, more answers. The harsh glare of a flash causing light to dance in front of her eyes. The press always terrified her. She could remember her father's constant instructions: Don't say any more than absolutely necessary. Don't let them see what you're feeling. They'll devour you.

Churning inside, Asher faced the pack of avid reporters with apparent ease. Her voice was quiet and assured. Her fingers were locked tightly together. With a smile she glanced quickly down the hall, searching for an escape route. Ty leaned negligently against the wall and gave her no assistance.

"Will your father be in Rome to watch you play?"

"Possibly." An ache, a sadness, carefully concealed.

"Did you divorce Lord Wickerton so you could play again?"

"My divorce has nothing to do with my profession." A half-truth, a lingering anger, smoothly disguised.

"Are you nervous about facing young rackets like Kingston and old foes like Martinelli?"

"I'm looking forward to it." A terror, a well of doubts, easily masked.

"Will you and Starbuck pair up again?"

Fury, briefly exposed.

"Starbuck's a singles player," she managed after a moment.

"You guys'll have to keep your eyes open to see if that changes." With his own brand of nonchalance, Ty slipped an arm around Asher's rigid shoulders. "There's no telling what might happen, is there, Asher?"

Her answer was an icy smile. "You've always been more unpredictable than I have, Ty."

He met the smile with one of his own. "Have I?" Leaning down, he brushed her lips lightly. Flashbulbs popped in a blaze of excitement. Even as their lips met, so did their eyes. Hers were twin slits of fury, his grimly laughing and ripe with purpose. Lazily he straightened. "The Face and I have some catching up to do."

"In Rome?" a reporter cracked.

Ty grinned and quite deliberately drew Asher closer. "That's where it started."

Chapter Two

*R*ome. The Colosseum. The Trevi fountain. The Vatican. Ancient history, tragedy and triumphs. Gladiators and competition. In the Foro Italico the steaming Italian sun beat down on the modern-day competitors just as it had on those of the Empire. To play in this arena was a theatrical experience. It was sun and space. There were lush umbrella pines and massive statues to set the forum apart from any other on the circuit. Beyond the stadium, wooded hills rose from the Tiber. Within its hedge trimmings, ten thousand people could chant, shout and whistle. Italian tennis fans were an emotional, enthusiastic and blatantly patriotic lot. Asher hadn't forgotten.

Nor had she forgotten that the Foro Italico had been the setting for the two biggest revelations in her life: her consuming love for tennis, her overwhelming love for Ty Starbuck.

She had been seven the first time she had watched her father win the Italian championship in the famed *campo central*. Of course she had seen him play before. One of her earliest memories was of watching her tall, tanned father dash around a court in blazing white. Jim Wolfe had been a champion before Asher had been born, and a force to be reckoned with long after.

Her own lessons had begun at the age of three. With her shortened racket she had hit balls to some of the greatest players of her father's generation. Her looks and her poise had made her a pet among the athletes. She grew up finding nothing unusual about seeing her picture in the paper or bouncing on the knee of a Davis Cup champion. Tennis and travel ruled her world. She had napped in the rear of limousines and walked across the pampered grass of Wimbledon. She had curtsied to heads of state and had her cheek pinched by a president. Before she began attending school she had already crossed the Atlantic a half dozen times.

But it had been in Rome, a year after the death of her mother, that Asher Wolfe had found a life's love and ambition.

Her father had still been wet and glowing from his victory, his white shorts splattered with the red dust of the court, when she had told him she would play in the *campo central* one day. And win.

Perhaps it had been a father's indulgence for his only child, or his ambition. Or perhaps it had been the quietly firm determination he saw in seven-year-old eyes. But Asher's journey had begun that day, with her father as her guide and her mentor.

Fourteen years later, after her own defeat in the semi-finals, Asher had watched Starbuck's victory. There had been nothing similar in the style of her father and the style of the new champion. Jim Wolfe had played a meticulous game—cold control with the accent on form. Starbuck played like a fireball—all emotion and muscle. Often, Asher had speculated on what the results would be if the two men were to meet across a net. Where her father brought her pride, Ty brought her excitement. Watching him, she could understand the sense of sexuality onlookers experienced during a bullfight. Indeed, there was a thirst for blood in his style that both alarmed and fascinated.

Ty had pursued her doggedly for months, but she had held him off. His reputation with women, his temper, his flamboyance and nonconformity had both attracted and repulsed her. Though the attraction was strong, and her heart was already lost, Asher had sensibly listened to her head. Until that day in May.

He'd been like a god, a powerful, mythological warrior with a strength and power that even the biased Italian crowd couldn't resist. Some cheered him, some cheerfully cursed him. He'd given them the sweat they had come to see. And the show.

Ty had taken the championship in seven frenzied sets. That night Asher had given him both her innocence and her love. For the first time in her life she had allowed her heart complete freedom. Like a blossom kept in the sheltered, controlled climate of a hothouse, she took to the sun and storm wildly. Days were steamier and more passionate—nights both turbulent and tender. Then the season had ended.

Now, as Asher practiced in the early morning lull on court five, the memories stirred, sweet and bitter as old wine. Fast rides on back roads, hot beaches, dim hotel rooms, foolish laughter, crazy loving. Betrayal.

"If you dream like that this afternoon, Kingston's going to wipe you out of the quarter-finals."

At the admonishment, Asher snapped back. "Sorry."

"You should be, when an old lady drags herself out of bed at six to hit to you."

Asher laughed. At thirty-three, Madge Haver-beck was still a force to be reckoned with across a net. Small and stocky, with flyaway brown hair and comfortably attractive features, she looked like an ad for home-baked cookies. She was, in fact, a world-class player with two Wimbledon champion-ships, a decade of other victories that included the Wightman Cup and a wicked forehand smash. For two years Asher had been her doubles partner to their mutual satisfaction and success. Her husband was a sociology professor at Yale whom Madge affectionately termed "The Dean."

"Maybe you should sit down and have a nice cup of tea," Asher suggested while tucking her tongue in her cheek. "This game's rough on middle-aged matrons."

After saying something short and rude, Madge sent a bullet over the net. Light and agile, Asher sprang after it. Her concentration focused. Her muscles went to work. In the drowsy morning hum the ball thudded on clay and twanged off strings. Madge wasn't a woman to consider a practice work-out incidental. She hustled over the court, driving Asher back to the baseline, luring her to the net, hammering at her by mixing her shots while Asher concentrated on adjusting her pace to the slow, frustrating clay.

For a fast, aggressive player, the surface could be deadly. It took strength and endurance rather than speed. Asher thanked the endless hours of weight lifting as she swung the racket again and again. The muscles in the slender arm were firm.

After watching one of Asher's returns scream past, Madge shifted her racket to her left hand. "You're pretty sharp for three years off, Face."

Asher filled her lungs with air. "I've kept my hand in."

Though Madge wondered avidly about Asher's marriage and years of self-imposed retirement, she knew her former partner too well to question. "Kingston hates to play the net. It's her biggest weakness."

"I know." Asher slipped the spare ball in her pocket. "I've studied her. Today she's going to play my game."

"She's better on clay than grass."

It was a roundabout way of reminding Asher of her own weakness. She gave Madge one of her rare, open smiles. "It won't matter. Next week I'm play-ing center court."

Slipping on a warm-up jacket, Madge gave a

hoot of laughter. "Haven't changed much, have you?"

"Bits and pieces." Asher dabbed at sweat with her wristband. "What about you? How're you going to play Fortini?"

"My dear." Madge fluffed at her hair. "I'll simply overpower her."

Asher snorted as they strolled off the court. "You haven't changed either."

"If you'd told me you were coming back," Madge put in, "we'd be playing doubles. Fisher's good, and I like her, but . . ."

"I couldn't make the decision until I was sure I wouldn't make a fool of myself." Slowly Asher flexed her racket arm. "Three years, Madge. I ache." She sighed with the admission. "I don't remember if I ached like this before."

"We can trade legs any time you say, Face."

Remembering, Asher turned with a look of concern. "How's the knee?"

"Better since the surgery last year." Madge shrugged. "I can still forecast rain though. Here's to a sunny season."

"I'm sorry I wasn't there for you."

Madge hooked her arm through Asher's in easy comradeship. "Naturally I expected you to travel six thousand miles to hold my hand."

"I would have if . . ." Asher trailed off, remembering the state of her marriage at the time of Madge's surgery.

Recognizing guilt, Madge gave Asher a friendly nudge with her elbow. "It wasn't as big a deal as the press made out. Of course," she added with a grin,

"I milked it for a lot of sympathy. The Dean brought me breakfast in bed for two months. Bless his heart."

"Then you came back and demolished Rayski in New York."

"Yeah." Madge laughed with pleasure. "I enjoyed that."

Asher let her gaze wander over the serene arena, quiet but for the thud of balls and hum of bees. "I have to win this one, Madge. I need it. There's so much to prove."

"To whom?"

"Myself first." Asher moved her shoulders restlessly, shifting her bag to her left hand. "And a few others."

"Starbuck? No, don't answer," Madge continued, seeing Asher's expression out of the corner of her eye. "It just sort of slipped out."

"What was between Ty and me was finished three years ago," Asher stated, deliberately relaxing her muscles.

"Too bad." Madge weathered Asher's glare easily. "I like him."

"Why?"

Stopping, Madge met the direct look. "He's one of the most alive people I know. Ever since he learned to control his temper, he brings so much emotion to the courts. It's good for the game. You don't have a stale tournament when Starbuck's around. He also brings that same emotion into his friendships."

"Yes," Asher agreed. "It can be overwhelming."

"I didn't say he was easy," Madge countered. "I

said I liked him. He is exactly who he is. There isn't a lot of phony business to cut through to get to Starbuck." Madge squinted up at the sun. "I suppose some of it comes from the fact that we turned pro the same year, did our first circuit together. Anyway, I've watched him grow from a cocky kid with a smart mouth to a cocky man who manages to keep that wicked temper just under the surface."

"You like him for his temper?"

"Partly." The mild, homey-looking woman smiled. "Starbuck's just plain strung right, Asher. He's not a man you can be ambivalent about. You're either for him or against him."

It was as much inquiry as statement. Saying nothing, Asher began to walk again. Ambivalence had never entered into her feeling for Ty.

On his way back from his own practice court Ty watched them. More accurately he watched Asher. While she remained unaware of him, he could take in every detail. The morning sun glinted down on her hair. Her shoulders were strong and slender, her gait long, leggy and confident. He was grateful he could study her now with some dispassion.

When he had looked out and had seen her in the stands two weeks before, it had been like catching a fast ball with his stomach. Shimmering waves of pain, shock, anger, one sensation had raced after the other. He had blown the first set.

Then he had done more than pull himself together. He had used the emotions against his opponent. The Frenchman hadn't had a chance against Ty's skill combined with three years of pent-up fury. Always, he played his best under pressure and stress.

It fed him. With Asher in the audience the match had become a matter of life and death. When she had left him she'd stolen something from him. Somehow, the victory had helped him regain a portion of it.

Damn her that she could still get to him. Ty's thoughts darkened as the distance between them decreased. Just looking at her made him want.

He had wanted her when she had been seventeen. The sharp, sudden desire for a teenager had astonished the then twenty-three-year-old Ty. He had kept a careful distance from her all that season. But he hadn't stopped wanting her. He had done his best to burn the desire out by romancing women he considered more his style—flamboyant, reckless, knowledgeable.

When Asher had turned twenty-one Ty had abandoned common sense and had begun a determined, almost obsessive pursuit. The more she had evaded him, the firmer she refused, the stronger his desire had grown. Even the victory, tasted first in Rome, hadn't lessened his need.

His life, which previously had had one focus, then had realigned with two dominating forces. Tennis and Asher. At the time he wouldn't have said he loved tennis, but simply that it was what and who he was. He wouldn't have said he loved Asher, but merely that he couldn't live without her.

Yet he had had to—when she'd left him to take another man's name. A title and a feather bed, Ty thought grimly. He was determined to make Asher Wolfe pay for bringing him a pain he had never expected to feel.

By turning left and altering his pace Ty cut across her path, apparently by chance. "Hi, Madge." He gave the brunette a quick grin, flicking his finger down her arm before turning his attention fully to Asher.

"Hiya, Starbuck." Madge glanced from the man to the woman and decided she wasn't needed. "Hey, I'm late," she said by way of explanation, then trotted off. Neither Asher nor Ty commented.

From somewhere in the surrounding trees Asher heard the high clear call of a bird. Nearer at hand was the slumberous buzz of bees and dull thud of balls. On court three, someone cursed fluently. But Asher was conscious only of Ty beside her.

"Just like old times," he murmured, then grinned at her expression. "You and Madge," he added.

Asher struggled not to be affected. The setting had too many memories. "She hit to me this morning. I hope I don't have to face her in the tournament."

"You go against Kingston today."

"Yes."

He took a step closer. In her mind's eye Asher saw the hedge beside her. With Ty directly in her path, dignified retreat was impossible. For all her delicacy of looks, Asher didn't run from a battle. She linked her fingers, then dragged them apart, annoyed.

"And you play Devoroux."

His acknowledgment was a nod. "Is your father coming?"

"No." The answer was flat and brief. Ty had never been one to be put off by a subtle warning.

"Why?"

"He's busy." She started to move by him, but succeeded only in closing the rest of the distance between them. Maneuvering was one of the best aspects of Ty's game.

"I've never known him to miss one of your major tournaments." In an old habit he couldn't resist nor she prevent, he reached for her hair. "You were always his first order of business."

"Things change," she responded stiffly. "People change."

"So it seems." His grin was sharp and cocky. "Will your husband be here?"

"Ex-husband." Asher tossed her head to dislodge his hand. "And no."

"Funny, as I recall he was very fond of tennis." Casually he set down his bag. "Has that changed too?"

"I need to shower." Asher had drawn nearly alongside of him before Ty stopped her. His hand slipped to her waist too quickly and too easily.

"How about a quick set for old time's sake?"

His eyes were intense—that oddly compelling color that was half night and half day. Asher remembered how they seemed to darken from the pupils out when he was aroused. The hand at her waist was wide-palmed and long-fingered—a concert pianist's hand, but it was rough and worked. The strength in it would have satisfied a prizefighter.

"I don't have time." Asher pushed to free herself and connected with the rock-hard muscles of his forearm. She pulled her fingers back as though she'd been burned.

"Afraid?" There was mockery and a light threat

with the overtones of sex. Her blood heated to the force she had never been able to fully resist.

"I've never been afraid of you." And it was true enough. She had been fascinated.

"No?" He spread his fingers, drawing her an inch closer. "Fear's one of the popular reasons for running away."

"I didn't run," she corrected him. "I left." *Before you did,* she added silently. For once, she had outmaneuvered him.

"You still have some questions to answer, Asher." His arm slid around her before she could step back. "I've waited a long time for the answers."

"You'll go on waiting."

"For some," he murmured in agreement. "But I'll have the answer to one now."

She saw it coming and did nothing. Later she would curse herself for her passivity. But when he lowered his mouth to hers, she met it without resistance. Time melted away.

He had kissed her like this the first time—slowly, thoroughly, gently. It was another part of the enigma that a man so full of energy and turbulence could show such sensitivity. His mouth was exactly as Asher remembered. Warm, soft, full. Perhaps she had been lost the first time he had kissed her—drawn to the fury—captured by the tenderness. Even when he brought her closer, deepening the kiss with a low-throated groan, the sweetness never diminished.

As a lover he excelled because beneath the brash exterior was an underlying and deep-rooted respect for femininity. He enjoyed the softness, tastes and textures of women, and instinctively sought to bring them pleasure in lovemaking. As an inherent loner, it was another contradiction that Ty saw a lover as a partner, never a means to an end. Asher had sensed this from the first touch so many years ago. Now she let herself drown in the kiss with one final coherent thought. It had been so long.

Her arm, which should have pushed him away, curved up his back instead until her hand reached his shoulders. Her fingers grasped at him. Unhesitatingly she pressed her body to his. He was the one man who could touch off the passion she had so carefully locked inside. The only man who had ever reached her core and gained true intimacy—the meeting of minds as well as of bodies. Starved for the glimpses of joy she remembered, Asher clung while her mouth moved avidly on his. Her greed for more drove away all her reserve, and all her promises.

Oh, to be loved again, truly loved, with none of the emptiness that had haunted her life for too long! To give herself, to take, to know the pure, searing joy of belonging! The thoughts danced in her mind like dreams suddenly remembered. With a moan, a sigh, she pressed against him, hungry for what had been.

The purpose of the kiss had been to punish, but he'd forgotten. The hot-blooded passion that could spring from the cool, contained woman had forced all else from his mind but need. He needed her, still needed her, and was infuriated. If they had been alone, he would have taken her and then faced the consequences. His impulses were still difficult to control. But they weren't alone. Some small part of his mind clung to reality even while his body pulsed.

She was soft and eager. Everything he had ever wanted. All he had done without. Ty discovered he had gotten more answers than he'd bargained for.

Drawing her away, he took his time studying her face. Who could resist the dangerous power of a hurricane? The wicked, primitive rumblings of a volcano? She stared at him, teetering between sanity and desire.

Her eyes were huge and aware, her lips parted breathlessly. It was a look he remembered. Long nights in her bed, hurried afternoons or lazy mornings, she would look at him so just before loving. Hot and insistent, desire spread, then closed like a fist in his stomach. He stepped back so that they were no longer touching.

"Some things change," he remarked. "And some things don't," he added before turning to walk away.

There was time for deep breathing before Asher took her position for the first serve. It wasn't the thousand pairs of eyes watching around the court that had her nerves jumping. It was one pair, dark brown and intense, seventy-eight feet away. Stacie Kingston, age twenty, hottest newcomer to the game in two years. She had energy, force and drive, along with a fierce will to win. Asher recognized her very well. The red clay spread out before her, waiting.

Because she knew the importance of mastering the skittish nerves and flood of doubts, she continued to take long, deep breaths. Squeezing the small white ball, Asher discovered the true meaning of trial by fire. If she won, here where she had never won before, three years after she had last lifted a racket professionally, she would have passed the test. Rome, it seemed, would always be her turning point.

Because it was the only way, she blocked out the past, blocked out tomorrow and focused wholly on the contest. Tossing the ball up, she watched the ascent, then struck home. Her breath came out in a hiss of effort.

Kingston played a strong, offensive game. A studied, meticulous player, she understood and used the personality of clay to her advantage, forcing Asher to the baseline again and again. Asher found the dirt frustrating. It cut down on her speed. She was hurrying, defending herself. The awareness of this only made her rush more. The ball eluded her, bouncing high over her head when she raced to the net, dropping lazily into the forecourt when she hugged the baseline. Unnerved by her own demons, she double-faulted. Kingston won the first game, breaking Asher's serve and allowing her only one point.

The crowd was vocal, the sun ferocious. The air was thick with humidity. From the other side of the hedge Asher could hear the games and laughter of schoolchildren. She wanted to throw aside her racket and walk off the court. It was a mistake, a mistake, her mind repeated, to have come back. Why had she subjected herself to this again? To the effort and pain and humiliation?

Her face was utterly passive, showing none of the turmoil. Gripping the racket tightly, she fought off the weakness. She had played badly, she knew, because she had permitted Kingston to set the pace.

It had taken Asher less than six minutes from first service to defeat. Her skin wasn't even damp. She hadn't come back to give up after one game, nor had she come back to be humiliated. The stands were thick with people watching, waiting. She had only herself.

Flicking a hand at the short skirt of her tennis dress, she walked back to the baseline. Crouched, she shifted her weight to the balls of her feet. Anger with herself was forced back. Fear was conquered. A cool head was one of her greatest weapons, and one she hadn't used in the first game. This time, she was determined. This time, the game would be played her way.

She returned the serve with a drop shot over the net that caught Kingston off balance. The crowd roared its approval as the ball boy scurried across the court to scoop up the dead ball.

Love–fifteen. Asher translated the scoring in her head with grim satisfaction. Fear had cost her the first game. Now, in her own precise way, she was out for blood. Kingston became more symbol than opponent.

Asher continued to draw her opponent into the net, inciting fierce volleys that brought the crowd to its feet. The roar and babble of languages did not register with her. She saw only the ball, heard only the effortful breathing that was hers. She ended that volley with a neatly placed ball that smacked clean at the edge of the baseline.

Something stirred in her—the hot, bubbling juice of victory. Asher tasted it, reveled in it as she walked coolly back to position. Her face was wet now, so she brushed her wristband over her brow before she cupped the two service balls in her hand. Only the beginning, she told herself. Each game was its own beginning.

By the end of the first set the court surface was zigzagged with skid marks. Red dust streaked the snowy material of her dress and marked her shoes. Sweat rolled down her sides after thirty-two minutes of ferocious play. But she'd taken the first set six–three.

Adrenaline was pumping madly, though Asher looked no more flustered than a woman about to hostess a dinner party. The competitive drives she had buried were in complete control. Part of her sensed Starbuck was watching. She no longer cared. At that moment Asher felt that if she had faced him across the net, she could have beaten him handily. When Kingston returned her serve deep, Asher met it with a topspin backhand that brushed the top of the net. Charging after the ball, she met the next return with a powerful lob.

The sportswriters would say that it was at that moment, when the two women were eye to eye, that Asher won the match. They remained that way for seconds only, without words, but communication had been made. From then Asher dominated, forcing Kingston into a defensive game. She set a merciless pace. When she lost a point she came back to take two. The aggressiveness was back, the cold-blooded warfare the sportswriters remembered with pleasure from her early years on the court.

Where Starbuck was fire and flash, she was ice and control. Never once during a professional match had

Asher lost her iron grip on her temper. It had once been a game among the sportswriters—waiting for The Face to cut loose.

Only twice during the match did she come close to giving them satisfaction, once on a bad call and once on her own poor judgment of a shot. Both times she stared down at her racket until the urge to stomp and swear had passed. When she had again taken her position, there had been nothing but cool determination in her eyes.

She took the match six–one, six–two in an hour and forty-nine minutes. Twice she had held Kingston's service to love. Three times she had served aces—something Kingston with her touted superserve had been unable to accomplish. Asher Wolfe would go on to the semi-finals. She had made her comeback.

Madge dropped a towel over Asher's shoulders as she collapsed on her chair. "Good God, you were terrific! You destroyed her." Asher said nothing, covering her face with the towel a moment to absorb sweat. "I swear, you're better than you were before."

"She wanted to win," Asher murmured, letting the towel drop limply again. "I *had* to win."

"It showed," Madge agreed, giving her shoulder a quick rub. "Nobody'd believe you haven't played pro in three years. I hardly believe it myself."

Slowly Asher lifted her face to her old partner. "I'm not in shape yet, Madge," she said beneath the din of the still-cheering crowd. "My calves are knotted. I don't even know if I can stand up again."

Madge skimmed a critical glance over Asher's

features. She couldn't detect a flicker of pain. Bending, she scooped up Asher's warm-up jacket, then draped it over Asher's shoulders. "I'll help you to the showers. I don't play for a half hour. You just need a few minutes on the massage table."

Exhausted, hurting, Asher started to agree, then spotted Ty watching her. His grin might have been acknowledgment of her victory. But he knew her, Asher reflected, knew her inside as no one else did.

"No thanks, I'll manage." Effortfully she rose to zip the cover around her racket. "I'll see you after you beat Fortini."

"Asher—"

"No, really, I'm fine now." Head high, muscles screaming, she walked toward the tunnel that led to the locker rooms.

Alone in the steam of the showers, Asher let herself empty, weeping bitterly for no reason she could name.

Chapter Three

It was the night after her victory in the semi-finals that Asher confronted Ty again. She had kept herself to a rigorous schedule of practice, exercise, press and play. Her pacing purposely left her little time for recreation. Practice was a religion. Morning hours were spent in the peaceful tree-shaded court five, grooving in, polishing her footwork, honing her reflexes.

Exercise was a law. Push-ups and weight lifting, stretching and hardening the muscles. Good press was more than a balm for the ego. Press was important to the game as a whole as well as the individual player. And the press loved a winner.

Play was what the athlete lived for. Pure competition—the testing of the skills of the body, the use of the skills of the mind. The best played as the best dancers danced—for the love of it. During the days of her second debut, Asher rediscovered love.

In her one brief morning meeting with Ty she had rediscovered passion. Only her fierce concentration on her profession kept her from dwelling on a need that had never died. Rome was a city for lovers—it had been once for her. Asher knew that this time she must think of it only as a city for competiton if she was to survive the first hurdle of regaining her identity. Lady Wickerton was a woman she hardly recognized. She had nearly lost Asher Wolfe trying to fit an image. How could she recapture herself if she once again became Starbuck's lady?

In a small club in the Via Sistina where the music was loud and the wine was abundant, Asher sat at a table crowded with bodies. Elbows nudged as glasses were reached for. Liquor spilled and was cheerfully cursed. In the second and final week of the Italian Open, the tension grew, but the pace mercifully slowed.

Rome was noise, fruit stands, traffic, outdoor cafés. Rome was serenity, cathedrals, antiquity. For the athletes it was days of grueling competition and nights of celebration or commiseration. The next match was a persistent shadow over the thoughts of the winners and the losers. As the music blared and the drinks were poured, they discussed every serve, every smash and error and every bad call. Rome was blissfully indolent over its reputation for bad calls.

"Long!" A dark, lanky Australian brooded into his wine. "That ball was inside by two inches. Two bloody inches."

"You won the game, Michael," Madge reminded

him philosophically. "And in the second game of the fifth set, you had a wide ball that wasn't called."

The Australian grinned and shrugged. "It was only a little wide." He brought his thumb and forefinger close together at the good-natured razzing of his peers. "What about this one?" His gesture was necessarily shortened by the close quarters as he lifted a drink toward Asher. "She beats an Italian in the Foro Italico, and the crowd still cheers her."

"Breeding," Asher returned with a mild smile. "The fans always recognize good breeding."

Michael snorted before he swallowed the heavy red wine. "Since when does a bloody steamroller need breeding?" he countered. "You flattened her." To emphasize his point he slammed a palm down on the table and ground it in.

"Yeah." Her smile widened in reminiscent pleasure. "I did, didn't I?" She sipped her dry, cool wine. The match had been longer and more demanding than her first with Kingston, but her body had rebelled a bit less afterward. Asher considered it a double victory.

"Tia Conway will go for your jugular," he said pleasantly, then called to his countrywoman at a nearby table. "Hey, Tia, you gonna beat this nasty American?"

A dark, compact woman with striking black eyes glanced over. The two women measured each other slowly before Tia lifted her glass in salute. Asher responded in kind before the group fell back to its individual conversations. With the music at high volume, they shouted to be heard, but words carried only a foot.

"A nice woman," Michael began, "off the court. On it, she's a devil. Off, she grows petunias and rosemary. Her husband sells swimming pools."

Madge chuckled. "You make that sound like a misdemeanor."

"I bought one," he said ruefully, then looked back at Asher. She was listening with half an ear to the differing opinions on either side of her of a match by two players. "Still, if I played mixed doubles, I'd want Face for a partner." Asher acknowledged this with a curious lift of a brow. "Tia plays like a demon, but you have better court sense. And," he added as he downed more wine, "better legs."

For this Madge punched him in the shoulder. "What about me?"

"You have perhaps the best court sense of any female world-class player," Michael decided slowly. "But," he continued as Madge accepted her due with a regal nod, "you have legs like a shot-putter."

A roar of laughter rose up over Madge's indignation. Asher leaned back in her chair, enjoying the loosening freedom of mirth as Madge challenged Michael to show his own and be judged. At that moment Asher's eyes locked with Ty's. Her laughter died unnoticed by her companions.

He'd come in late and alone. His hair was unruly, as though he had ridden in a fast car with the top down. Even completely relaxed, dressed in jeans, his hands in his pockets, some aura of excitement swirled around him. In the dim light his face was shadowed, all hollows and planes, with his eyes dark and knowing. No woman could be immune to him.

A former lover was helpless not to remember what magic his mouth could perform.

Asher sat still as a stone—marble, pale and elegant in the rowdy, smoke-curtained bar. She couldn't forget any more than she could stop wanting. All she could do was refuse, as she had three years before.

Without taking his eyes from hers Ty crossed the room, skirting crowded tables. He had Asher by the arm, drawing her to her feet before the rest of the group had greeted him.

"We'll dance." It was a command formed in the most casual tones. As on court, Asher's decision had to be made in a tenth of a second. To refuse would have incited speculative gossip. To agree meant she had her own demons to deal with.

"I'd love to," she said coolly, and went with him.

The band played a slow ballad at ear-splitting volume. The vocalist was flat, and tried to make up for it by being loud. Someone knocked a glass off a table with a splintering crash. There was a pungent scent of spilled wine. A bricklayer argued with a Mexican tennis champion on the proper way to handle a topspin lob. Someone was smoking a pipe filled with richly sweet cherry tobacco. The floorboards were slightly warped.

Ty gathered her into his arms as though she had never been away. "The last time we were here," he murmured in her ear, "we sat at that corner table and drank a bottle of Valpolicella."

"I remember."

"You wore the same perfume you're wearing now." His lips grazed her temple as he drew her closer. Asher felt the bones in her legs liquefy, the muscles in her thighs loosen. "Like sun-warmed petals." Her heartbeat was a light, uncertain flutter against his. "Do you remember what we did afterward?"

"We walked."

The two hoarsely spoken words seemed to shiver along his skin. It was impossible to keep his mouth from seeking small tastes of her. "Until sunrise." His breath feathered intimately at her ear. "The city was all rose and gold, and I wanted you so badly, I nearly exploded. You wouldn't let me love you then."

"I don't want to go back." Asher tried to push away, but his arms kept her pressed tight against him. It seemed every line of his body knew every curve of hers.

"Why? Because you might remember how good we were together?"

"Ty, stop it." She jerked her head back—a mistake as his lips cruised lazily over hers.

"We'll be together again, Asher." He spoke quietly. The words seemed to sear into the tender flesh of her lips. "Even if it's only once . . . for old time's sake."

"It's over, Ty." The claim was a whisper, the whisper unsteady.

"Is it?" His eyes darkened as he pressed her against him almost painfully. "Remember, Asher, I know you, inside out. Did your husband ever find out who you really are? Did he know how to make you laugh? How," he added in a low murmur, "to make you moan?"

She stiffened. The music whirled around them,

fast now with an insistent bass beat. Ty held her firmly against him, barely swaying at all. "I won't discuss my marriage with you."

"I damn well don't want to know about your *marriage*." He said the word as if it were an obscenity as his fingers dug into the small of her back. Fury was taking over though he'd sworn he wouldn't let it. He could still get to her. Yes, yes, that was a fact, he knew, but no more than she could still get to him. "Why did you come back?" he demanded. "Why the hell did you come back?"

"To play tennis." Her fingers tightened on his shoulder. "To win." Anger was growing in her as well. It appeared he was the only man who could make her forget herself enough to relinquish control. "I have every right to be here, every right to do what I was trained to do. I don't owe you explanations."

"You owe me a hell of a lot more." It gave him a certain grim satisfaction to see the fury in her eyes. He wanted to push. Wanted to see her anger. "You're going to pay for the three years you played lady of the manor."

"You don't know anything about it." Her breath came short and fast. Her eyes were nearly cobalt. "I paid, Starbuck, I paid more than you can imagine. Now I've finished, do you understand?" To his surprise, her voice broke on a sob. Quickly she shook her head and fought back tears. "I've finished paying for my mistakes."

"What mistakes?" he demanded. Frustrated, he took her by the shoulders. "What mistakes, Asher?"

"You." She drew in her breath sharply, as if stepping back from a steep edge. "Oh, God, you."

Turning, she fought her way through the swarm of enthusiastic dancers. Even as she sprang out into the sultry night Ty whirled her around. "Let me go!" She struck out blindly, but he grabbed her wrist.

"You're not going to walk out on me again." His voice was dangerously low. "Not ever again."

"Did it hurt your pride, Ty?" Emotion erupted from her, blazing as it could only from one who constantly denied it. "Did it hurt your ego that a woman could turn her back on you and choose someone else?"

Pain ripped through him and took over. "I never had your kind of pride, Asher." He dragged her against him, needing to prove he had some kind of power over her, even if it was only physical. "The kind you wear so that no one can see you're human. Did you run because I knew you? Because in bed I could make you forget to be the perfect lady?"

"I left because I didn't want you!" Completely unstrung, she shouted, pounding with her free hand. "I didn't want—"

He cut her off with a furious kiss. Their tempers soared into vivid passion. Anger sizzled in two pairs of lips that clung because they were helpless to do otherwise. There was never any choice when they were together. It had been so almost from the first, and the years had changed nothing. She could resist him, resist herself, for only so long. The outcome was inevitable.

Suddenly greedy, Asher pressed against him. Here was the sound and the speed. Here was the storm. Here was home. His hair was thick and soft between her questing fingers, his body rock-hard against the firmness of hers. His scent was his "off-court" fragrance—something sharp and bracing that she'd always liked.

The first taste was never enough to satisfy her, so she probed deeper into his mouth, tongue demanding, teeth nipping in the way he himself had taught her. A loud crash of brass from the band rattled the windows behind them. Asher heard only Ty's moan of quiet desperation. Between the shadows and the moonlight they clung, passion building, old needs merging with new.

Her breath trembled into the night as he took a crazed journey of her face. His hands slid up until his thumbs hooked gently under her chin. It was a familiar habit, one of his more disarming. Asher whispered his name half in plea, half in acceptance before his mouth found hers again. He drew her into him, slowly, inevitably, while his fingers skimmed along her cheekbones. The more tempestuous the kiss, the more tender his touch. Asher fretted for the strong, sure stroke of his hands on her body.

Full circle, she thought dizzily. She had come full circle. But if once before in Rome she had been frightened when his kisses had drained and exhilarated her, now she was terrified.

"Please, Ty." Asher turned her head until her brow rested on his shoulder. "Please, don't do this."

"I didn't do it alone," he muttered.

Slowly she lifted her head. "I know."

It was the vulnerability in her eyes that kept him from dragging her back to him. Just as it had been her vulnerability all those years before that had prevented him from taking her. He had waited for her to come to him. The same would hold true this time, he realized. Cursing potently under his breath, Ty released her.

"You've always known how to hold me off, haven't you, Asher?"

Knowing the danger had passed, she let out an unsteady breath. "Self-preservation."

Ty gave an unexpected laugh as his hands dove for his pockets. "It might have been easier if you'd managed to get fat and ugly over the last three years. I wanted to think you had."

A hint of a smile played on her mouth. So his moods could change, she thought, just as quickly as ever. "Should I apologize for not accommodating you?"

"Probably wouldn't have made any difference if you had." His eyes met hers again, then roamed her face. "Just looking at you—it still takes my breath away." His hands itched to touch. He balled them into fists inside his pockets. "You haven't even changed your hair.

This time the smile bloomed. "Neither have you. You still need a trim."

He grinned. "You were always conservative."

"You were always unconventional."

He gave a low appreciative laugh, one she hadn't heard in much too long. "You've mellowed," he decided. "You used to say radical."

"*You've* mellowed," Asher corrected him. "It used to be true."

With a shrug he glanced off into the night. "I used to be twenty."

"Age, Starbuck?" Sensing a disturbance, Asher automatically sought to soothe it.

"Inevitably." He brought his eyes back to hers. "It's a young game."

"Ready for your rocking chair?" Asher laughed, forgetting caution as she reached up to touch his cheek. Though she snatched her hand away instantly, his eyes had darkened. "I—" She searched for a way to ease the fresh tension. "You didn't seem to have any problem smashing Bigelow in the semifinals. He's what, twenty-four?"

"It went to seven sets." His hand came out of his pocket. Casually he ran the back of it up her throat. "You like it best that way."

He felt her swallow quickly, nervously, though her eyes remained level. "Come back with me, Asher," he murmured. "Come with me now." It cost him to ask, but only he was aware of how much.

"I can't."

"Won't," he countered.

From down the street came a high-pitched stream of Italian followed by a bellow of laughter. Inside the club the band murdered a popular American tune. She could smell the heat-soaked fragrance of the window-box geraniums above their heads. And she could remember, remember too well, the sweetness that could be hers if she crossed the line. And the pain.

"Ty." Asher hesitated, then reached up to grasp the hand that lingered at her throat. "A truce, please. For our mutual benefit," she added when his fingers interlaced possessively with hers. "With us both going into the finals, we don't need this kind of tension right now."

"Save it for later?" He brought her reluctant hand to his lips, watching her over it. "Then we pick this up in Paris."

"I didn't mean—"

"We deal now or later, Face, but we deal." He grinned again, tasting challenge, tasting victory. "Take it or leave it."

"You're just as infuriating as ever."

"Yeah." The grin only widened. "That's what keeps me number one."

On an exasperated laugh, Asher let her hand relax in his. "Truce, Starbuck?"

He let his thumb glide back and forth over her knuckles. "Agreed, on one condition." Sensing her withdrawal, he continued. "One question, Asher. Answer one question."

She tried to wrest her hand away and failed. "What question?" she demanded impatiently.

"Were you happy?"

She became very still as quick flashes of the past raced through her head. "You have no right—"

"I have every right," he interrupted. "I'm going to know that, Asher. The truth."

She stared at him, wanting to pit her will against his. Abruptly she found she had no energy for it. "No," she said wearily. "No."

He should have felt triumph, and instead felt misery. Releasing her hand, he stared out at the street. "I'll get you a cab."

"No. No, I'll walk. I want to walk."

Ty watched her move into the flood of a streetlight and back into the dark. Then she was a shadow, disappearing.

The streets were far from empty. Traffic whizzed by at the pace that seemed the pride of European cities. Small, fast cars and daredevil taxis. People scattered the sidewalks, rushing toward some oasis of nightlife. Still, Ty thought he could hear the echo of his own footsteps.

Perhaps it was because so many feet had walked the Roman streets for so many centuries. Ty didn't care much for history or tradition. Tennis history perhaps—Gonzales, Gibson, Perry, these names meant more to him than Caesar, Cicero or Caligula. He rarely thought of his own past, much less of antiquity. Ty was a man who focused on the present. Until Asher had come back into his life, he had thought little about tomorrow.

In his youth he had concentrated fiercely on the future, and what he would do if . . . Now that he had done it, Ty had come to savor each day at a time. Still, the future was closing in on him, and the past was never far behind.

At ten he had been a hustler. Skinny and streetwise, he had talked his way out of trouble when it was possible, and slugged his way out when it wasn't. Growing up in the tough South Side of Chicago, Ty had been introduced to the seamier side of life early. He'd tasted his first beer when he should have been studying rudimentary math. What had saved him from succumbing to the streets was his dislike and distrust of organized groups. Gangs had held no appeal for Ty. He had no desire to lead or to follow. Still, he might have chosen a less honorable road had it not been for his unbending, unquestioning love for his family.

His mother, a quiet, determined woman who worked nights cleaning office buildings, was precious to him. His sister, four years his junior, was his pride and self-assumed responsibility. There was no father, and even the memory of him had faded before Ty reached mid-childhood. Always, he had considered himself the head of the family, with all the duties and rights that it entailed. No one corrected him. It was for his family that he studied and kept on the right side of the law—though he brushed the line occasionally. It was for them that he promised himself, when he was still too young to realize the full extent of his vow, to succeed. One day he would move them out, buy them a house, bring his mother up off her knees. The picture of how hadn't been clear, only the final result. The answer had been a ball and racket.

Ada Starbuck had given her son a cheap, nylon-stringed racket for his tenth birthday. The gift had been an impulse. She had been determined to give the boy something other than the necessary socks and underwear. The racket, such as it was, had been a gesture of hope. She could see too many of her neighbors' children fall into packs. Ty, she knew, was different. A loner. With the racket he could entertain himself. A baseball or football required someone to catch or pass. Now Ty could use a concrete wall as his partner. And so he did—at first for lack of something better to do. In the alley between apartment buildings he would smash the ball against a wall scrawled with spray paint. DIDI LOVES FRANK and other less romantic statements littered his playing field.

He enjoyed setting his own rhythm, enjoyed the steady thud, thump, smash he could make. When he became bored with the wall, he began haunting the neighborhood playground courts. There, he could watch teenagers or middle-aged weekenders scramble around the courts. He hustled pennies retrieving balls. Deciding he could do better than the people he watched, Ty badgered an older boy into a game.

His first experience on a court was a revelation. A human forced you to run, sent balls over your head or lined them at you with a speed a stationary wall couldn't match. Though he lost handily, Ty had discovered the challenge of competition. And the thirst to win.

He continued to haunt the courts, paying more attention to details. He began to select the players who took the game seriously. Possessing quite a bit of charm even at that age, Ty talked himself into more games. If someone took the time to teach, he listened and adjusted the advice to suit his own style. And he was developing a style. It was rough and untutored, with the flash the sportwriters would later rave about just a spark. His serve was a far cry from a grown Starbuck's, but it was strong and uncannily accurate. He was still awkward, as growing boys are, but his speed was excellent. More than anything else, his fierce desire to win had his game progressing.

When the cheap racket simply disintegrated under constant use, Ada raided the household budget and bought Ty another. Of the hundreds of rackets he had used in his career, some costing more than his mother had made in a week, Ty had never forgotten that first one. He had kept it, initially from childhood sentiment, then as a symbol.

He carved out a name for himself in the neighborhood. By the time he was thirteen it was a rare thing for anyone, child or adult, to beat Ty Starbuck on the courts. He knew his game. He had read everything he could get his hands on—tennis as a sport, its history, its great players. When his contemporaries were immersed in the progress of the White Sox or the Cubs, Ty watched the Wimbledon matches on the flickering black and white TV in his apartment. He had already made up his mind to be there one day. And to win. Again, it was Ada who helped the hand of fate.

One of the offices she cleaned belonged to Martin Derick, a lawyer and tennis enthusiast who patronized a local country club. He was an offhandedly friendly man whose late hours brought him in contact with the woman who scrubbed the hall outside his door. He called her Mrs. Starbuck because her dignity demanded it, and would exchange a word or greeting on his way in or out. Ada was careful to mention her son and his tennis abilities often enough to intrigue and not often enough to bore. Ty had come by his shrewdness naturally.

When Martin casually mentioned he would be interested in seeing the boy play, Ada told him there was an informal tournament set for that Saturday. Then she hurriedly arranged one. Whether curiosity or interest prompted Martin to drive to the battered

South Side court, the results were exactly as Ada hoped.

Ty's style was still rough, but it was aggressive. His temper added to the spark, and his speed was phenomenal. At the end of a set, Martin was leaning against the chain-link fence. At the end of the match, he was openly cheering. Two hours on the manicured courts of his club had never brought him quite this degree of excitement. Ideas humming in his brain, he walked over to the sweaty, gangly teenager.

"You want to play tennis, kid?"

Ty spun the racket as he eyed the lawyer's pricey suit. "You ain't dressed for it." He gave the smooth leather shoes a mild sneer.

Martin caught the insolent grin, but focused on the intensity of the boy's eyes. Some instinct told him they were champion's eyes. The ideas solidified into a goal. "You want to play for pay?"

Ty kept spinning the racket, wary of a hustle, but the question had his pulse leaping. "Yeah. So?"

This time Martin smiled at the deliberate rudeness. He was going to like this kid, God knew why. "So, you need lessons and a decent court." He glanced at Ty's worn racket. "And equipment. What kind of power can you get out of plastic strings?"

Defensive, Ty tossed up a ball and smashed it into the opposing service court.

"Not bad," Martin decided mildly. "You'd do better with sheep gut."

"Tell me something I don't know."

Martin drew out a pack of cigarettes and offered one to Ty. He refused with a shake of his head.

Taking his time, Martin lit one, then took a long drag.

"Those things'll mess up your lungs," Ty stated idly.

"Tell me something I don't know," the lawyer countered. "Think you can play on grass?"

Ty answered with a quick, crude expletive, then sliced another ball over the net.

"Pretty sure of yourself."

"I'm going to play Wimbledon," Ty told him matter-of-factly. "And I'm going to win."

Martin didn't smile, but reached into his pocket. He held out a discreet, expensively printed business card. "Call me Monday," he said simply, and walked away.

Ty had a patron.

The marriage wasn't made in heaven. Over the next seven years there were bitter arguments, bursts of temper and dashes of love. Ty worked hard because he understood that work and discipline were the means to the end. He remained in school and studied only because his mother and Martin had a conspiracy against him. Unless he completed high school with decent grades, the patronage would be removed. As to the patronage itself, Ty accepted it only because his needs demanded it. But he was never comfortable with it. The lessons polished his craft. Good equipment tightened his game. He played on manicured grass, well-tended clay and wood, learning the idiosyncrasies of each surface.

Every morning before school he practiced. Afternoons and weekends were dedicated to tennis. Summers, he worked part-time in the pro shop at

Martin's club, then used the courts to hone his skill. By the time he was sixteen the club's tennis pro could beat him only if Ty had an off day.

His temper was accepted. It was a game of histrionics. Women found a certain appeal in his lawlessness. Ty learned of female pleasures young, and molded his talent there as carefully as he did his game.

The only break in his routine came when he injured his hand coming to the defense of his sister. Ty considered the two-week enforced vacation worth it, as the boy Jess had been struggling with had a broken nose.

He traveled to his first tournament unknown and unseeded. In a lengthy, gritty match heralded in the sports pages, he found his first professional victory. When he lost, Ty was rude, argumentative and brooding. When he won, he was precisely the same. The press tolerated him because he was young, brilliant and colorful. His rise from obscurity was appreciated in a world where champions were bred in the affluent, select atmosphere of country clubs.

Before his nineteenth birthday Ty put a down payment on a three-bedroom house in a Chicago suburb. He moved his family out. When he was twenty he won his first Wimbledon title. The dream was realized, but his intensity never slackened.

Now, walking along the dark streets of Rome, he thought of his roots. Asher made him think of them, perhaps because hers were so markedly different. There had been no back alleys or street gangs in her life. Her childhood had been sheltered, privileged and rich. With James Wolfe as a father, her introduction to tennis had come much earlier and much easier than Ty's. At four she had a custom-made racket and had hit balls on her father's private courts. Her mother had hired maids to scrub floors, not been hired out to scrub them.

At times Ty wondered if it was that very difference that had attracted him to her. Then he would remember the way she felt in his arms. Backgrounds were blown to hell. Yet there was something about her reserve that had drawn him. That and the passion he had sensed lay beneath.

The challenge. Yes, Ty admitted with a frown, he was a man who couldn't resist a challenge. Something about the cool, distant Asher Wolfe had stirred his blood even when she had been little more than a child. He'd waited for her to grow up. And to thaw out, he reminded himself ruefully. Turning a corner without direction, Ty found himself approaching one of Rome's many fountains. The water twinkled with light gaiety while he watched, wishing his blood were as cool.

God, how he wanted her still. The need grated against pride, infuriating and arousing him. He would have taken her back that night even knowing she had been another man's wife, shared another man's bed. It would have been less difficult to have thought about her with many lovers than with one husband—that damn titled Englishman whose arms she had run to straight from his own. *Why?* The question pounded at him.

How many times in those first few months had he relived their last few days together, looking for the key? Then he'd layered over the hurt and the fury.

The wound had healed jaggedly, then callused. Ty had gone on because he was a survivor. He'd survived poverty, and the streets, and the odds. With an unsteady laugh he raked a hand through his thick mop of hair. But had he really survived Asher?

He knew he had taken more than one woman to bed because her hair was nearly the same shade, her voice nearly the same tone. Nearly, always nearly. Now, when he had all but convinced himself that what he remembered was an illusion, she was back. And free. Again, Ty laughed. Her divorce meant nothing to him. If she had still been legally tied to another man, it would have made no difference. He would still have taken her.

This time, he determined, he'd call the shots. He was out of patience. He would have her again, until he decided to walk away. Challenge, strategy, action. It was a course he had followed for half his life. Taking out a coin, he flipped it insolently into the rippling waters of a fountain, as if daring luck to evade him. It drifted down slowly until it nestled with a hundred other wishes.

His eyes skimmed the streets until he found the neon lights of a tiny bar. He wanted a drink.

Chapter Four

Asher had time to savor her title as Italian Woman's Champion on the flight between Rome and Paris. After the match she had been too exhausted from nearly two hours of unrelenting competition to react. She could remember Madge hugging her, the crowd cheering for her. She could remember the glare of flashbulbs in her face and the barrage of questions she had forced herself to answer before she all but collapsed on the massage table. Then the celebrations had run together in a blur of color and sound, interviews and champagne. Too many faces and handshakes and hugs. Too many reporters. Now, as the plane leveled, reaction set in. She'd done it.

For all of her professional career, the Italian clay had beaten her. Now—now her comeback was viable. She had proven herself. Every hour of strain, every moment of physical pain during the last six months of training had been worth it. At last Asher could rid herself of all the lingering doubts that she had made the right decision.

Though there had been no doubts about her choice to leave Eric, she mused, feeling little emotion at the dissolution of her marriage—a marriage, Asher remembered, that had been no more than a polite play after the first two months. If she had ever made a truly unforgivable mistake, it had been in marrying Lord Eric Wickerton.

All the wrong reasons, Asher reflected as she leaned back in her seat with her eyes closed. Even with her bitter thoughts of Eric, she could never remove the feeling of responsibility for taking the step that had legally bound them. He had known she hadn't loved him. It hadn't mattered to him. She had known he wanted her to fit the title of Lady. She hadn't cared. At the time the need to escape had been too overpowering. Asher had given Eric what he had wanted—a groomed, attractive wife and hostess. She had thought he would give her what she needed in return. Love and understanding. The reality had been much, much different, and almost as painful as what she had sought to escape. Arguments were more difficult, she had discovered, when two people had no mutual ground. And when one felt the other had sinned . . .

She wouldn't think of it, wouldn't think of the time in her life that had brought such pain and disillusionment. Instead, she would think of victory.

Michael had been right in his assessment of Tia on the court. She was a small, vibrant demon who played hard and never seemed to tire. Her skill was in picking holes in her opponent's game, then ruthlessly exploiting them. On court she wore gold—a thin chain around her neck, swinging hoops at her ears and a thick clip to tame her raven hair. Her dress was pastel and frilled. She played like an enraged tigress. Both women had run miles during the match, taking it to a full five sets. The last one had consisted of ten long, volatile games with the lead shooting back and forth as quickly as the ball. Never had it been more true that the match wasn't over until it was over.

And when it was over, both women had limped off the court, sweaty, aching and exhausted. But Asher had limped off with a title. Nothing else mattered.

Looking back on it, Asher found herself pleased that the match had been hard won. She wanted something the press would chatter about, something they would remember for more than a day or two. It was always news when an unseeded player won a world title—even considering Asher's record. As it was, her past only made her hotter copy. She needed that now to help keep the momentum going.

With Italy behind her, Paris was next. The first leg of the Grand Slam. She had won there before, on clay, the year she had been Starbuck's lady. As she had with Eric, Asher tried to block Ty out of her mind. Characteristically he wasn't cooperative.

We pick this up in Paris.

The words echoed softly in her head, part threat, part promise. Asher knew him too well to believe either was idle. She would have to deal with him when the time came. But she wasn't naïve or innocent any longer. Life had taught her there weren't any easy answers or fairy-tale endings. She'd lost too much to believe happy-ever-after waited at the end of every love affair—as she had once believed it had waited for her and Ty. They were no longer the prince and princess of the courts, but older, and, Asher fervently hoped, wiser.

She was certain he would seek to soothe his ego by trying to win her again—her body if not her heart. Remembering the verve and depth of his lovemaking, Asher knew it wouldn't be easy to resist him. If she could have done so without risking her emotions, Asher would have given Ty what he wanted. For three colorless years she had endured without the passion he had brought to her life. For three empty years she had wondered and wanted and denied.

But her emotions weren't safe. On a sigh, Asher allowed herself to feel. She still cared. Not a woman to lie to herself, Asher admitted she loved Ty, had never once stopped loving him. It had never been over for her, and deep within she carried the memory of that love. It brought guilt.

What if he had known? she thought with the familiar stir of panic. How could she have told him? Asher opened her eyes and stared blindly through the sunlight. It was as harsh and unforgiving as the emotions that raged through her. Would he have believed? Would he have accepted? Before the questions were fully formed, Asher shook her head in denial. He could never know that she had unwittingly married another man while she carried Ty's child. Or that through her own grief and despair she had lost that precious reminder of her love for him.

Closing her eyes, Asher willed herself to sleep. Paris was much too close.

"Ty! Ty!"

Pausing in the act of zipping the cover on his racket, Ty turned. Pleasure shot into his eyes. In a quick move he dropped his racket and grabbed the woman who had run to him. Holding her up, he whirled her in three dizzying circles before he crushed her against him. Her laughter bounced off the air in breathless gasps.

"You're breaking me!" she cried, but hugged him tighter.

Ty cut off her protest with a resounding kiss, then held her at arm's length. She was a small woman, nearly a foot shorter than he, nicely rounded without being plump. Her gray-green eyes were sparkling, her generous mouth curved in a dazzling smile. She was a beauty, he thought—had always been a beauty. Love surrounded him. He tousled her hair, dark as his own, but cut in a loose swinging style that brushed her shoulders. "Jess, what are you doing here?"

Grinning, she gave his ear a sisterly tug. "Being mauled by the world's top tennis player."

Ty slipped an arm around her shoulders, only then noticing the man who stood back watching them. "Mac." Keeping his arm around Jess, Ty extended a hand.

"Ty, how are you?"

"Fine. Just fine."

Mac accepted the handshake and careful greeting with light amusement. He knew how Ty felt about his little sister—the little sister who was now twenty-seven and the mother of his child. When he had married Jess, over two years before, Mac had understood that there was a bond between brother and sister that would not be severed. An only child, he both respected and envied it. Two years of being in-laws had lessened Ty's caution with him but hadn't alleviated it. Of course, Mac mused ruefully, it hadn't helped that he was fifteen years Jess's senior, or that he had moved her across the country to California, where he headed a successful research and development firm. And then, he preferred chess to tennis. He'd never have gotten within ten yards of Jessica Starbuck if he hadn't been Martin Derick's nephew.

Bless Uncle Martin, Mac thought with a glance at his lovely, adored wife. Ty caught the look and relaxed his grip on his sister. "Where's Pete?" he asked, making the overture by addressing Mac rather than his sister.

Mac acknowledged the gesture with a smile. "With Grandma. They're both pretty pleased with themselves."

Jess gave the bubbling laugh that both men loved. "Hardly more than a year old and he can move like lightning. Mom's thrilled to chase him around for a few weeks. She sends her love," she told Ty. "You know how she feels about long plane flights."

"Yeah." He released his sister to retrieve his bag

and racket. "I talked to her just last night; she didn't say anything about your coming."

"We wanted to surprise you." Smug, Jess hooked her hand into Mac's. "Mac thought Paris was the perfect place for a second honeymoon." She sent her husband a brief but intimate look. Their fingers tightened.

"The trick was getting her away from Pete for two weeks." He gave Ty a grin. "You were a bigger incentive than Paris." Bending, he kissed the top of his wife's head. "She dotes on Pete."

"No, I don't," Jess disagreed, then grinned. "Well, I wouldn't if Pete weren't such a smart baby."

Mac began to pack an old, favored pipe. "She's ready to enroll him in Harvard."

"Next year," Jess responded dryly. "So, you're going in as top seed," she continued, giving her full attention to her brother. Was there some strain around his eyes? she wondered, then quickly discounted it. "Martin's proud enough to bust."

"I was hoping he might make it out for the tournament." Ty glanced toward the empty stands. "Funny, I still have a habit of looking for him before a match."

"He wanted to be here. If there had been any way for him to postpone this trial, but . . ." Jess trailed off and smiled. "Mac and I will have to represent the family."

Ty slung the bag over his shoulder. "You'll do fine. Where are you staying?"

"At the—" Jess's words came to a stop as she

spotted a slender blonde crossing an empty court a short distance away. Reaching up, she brushed at her brow as if pushing aside an errant strand of hair. "Asher," she murmured.

Ty twisted his head. Asher wasn't aware of them, as Chuck was keeping her involved in what appeared to be a long, detailed description of a match. "Yes," Ty said softly. "Asher." He kept his eyes on her, watching the movements of her body beneath the loosely fitting jogging suit. "Didn't you know she was here?"

"Yes, I—" Jess broke off helplessly. How could she explain the flurry of feelings that she experienced in seeing Asher Wolfe again. The years were winked away in an instant. Jess could see the cool blue eyes, hear the firmly controlled voice. At the time there'd been no doubt in her mind about right and wrong. Even the chain reaction that had begun on a hazy September afternoon had only served to cement Jess's certainty. Now there'd been a divorce, and Asher was back. She felt her husband's warm palm against hers. Right and wrong weren't so clearly defined any longer.

A bubble of nausea rose as she turned to her brother. He was still watching Asher. Had he loved her? Did he still? What would he do if he ever learned of his sister's part in what had happened three years before? Jess found the questions trembling on her tongue and was afraid of the answers. "Ty . . ."

His eyes were dark and stormy, a barometer of emotion. Something in them warned Jess to keep her questions to herself. Surely there would be a better time to bring up the past. She had both a sense of reprieve and a feeling of guilt.

"Beautiful, isn't she?" he asked lightly. "Where did you say you were staying?"

"And because he's eighteen and played like a rocket in the qualifying rounds, they're muttering about an upset." Chuck tossed a tennis ball idly, squeezing it when it returned to his palm. "I wouldn't mind if he weren't such a little twerp."

Asher laughed and snatched the ball as Chuck tossed it again. "And eighteen," she added.

He gave a snort. "He wears designer underwear, for God's sake. His mother has them dry cleaned."

"Down boy," Asher warned good-naturedly. "You'll feel better once you wipe him out in the quarter-finals. Youth versus experience," she added because she couldn't resist. Chuck twisted a lock of her hair around his finger and pulled.

"You meet Rayski," he commented. "I guess we could call that two old pros."

Asher winced. "Your point," she conceded. "So, what's your strategy for this afternoon?"

"To beat the tar out of him," Chuck responded instantly, then grinned as he flexed his racket arm. "But if he gets lucky, I'll leave it up to Ty to smash him in the semis or the finals."

Asher bounced the ball on the clay. Her fingers closed over it, then released it again. "You're so sure Ty will get to the finals?"

"Money in the bank," he claimed. "This is his year. I swear, I've never seen him play better." Pleasure for his friend with the light lacing of envy gave the statement more impact. "He's going to be piling up titles like dominoes."

Asher said nothing, not even nodding in agreement as Chuck sought to prove his point by giving her a replay of Ty's qualifying match. A breeze stirred, sending blossoms drifting to the court at her feet. It was early morning, and the Stade Roland Garros was still drowsily charming and quiet. The thump of balls was hardly noticeable. In a few hours the fourteen thousand seats around the single center court would be jammed with enthusiasts. The noise would be human and emotional, accented by the sounds of traffic and squealing brakes on the highway that separated the stadium from the Bois de Boulogne.

Asher watched the breeze tickle a weeping willow as Chuck continued his rundown. In this first week of the games, tennis would be played for perhaps eleven hours a day so that even the first-round losers used the courts enough to make the trip worthwhile. It was considered by most pros the toughest championship to win. Like Ty, Asher was after her second victory.

Paris. Ty. Was there nowhere she could go that wasn't so firmly tied in with memories of him? In Paris they'd sat in the back of a darkened theater, necking like teenagers while an Ingmar Bergman film had flickered on the screen unnoticed. In Paris he had doctored a strained muscle in her calf, pampering and bullying so that she had won despite the pain. In Paris they had made love, and made love, and made love until they were both weak and exhausted. In Paris Asher had still believed in happy endings.

Fighting off memories, Asher glanced around the stadium. Her eyes locked with Jess's. Separated by a hundred yards, both women endured a jolt of shock and distress. They stared, unable to communicate, unable to look away.

"Hey, it's Jess!" Chuck interrupted himself to make the announcement. He waved, then grabbed Asher's hand to drag her with him. "Let's go say hi."

Panicked, Asher dug in her heels. "No, I—I have to meet . . ." Her mind was devoid of excuses, but she snatched her hand from Chuck's. "You go ahead, I'll see you later." Over Chuck's protests, she dashed in the opposite direction.

Breathless, Asher found herself in the Jardin des Plantes with its sweet, mingling scents, little plaques and poetry. It seemed an odd setting for jangled nerves. Making an effort to calm herself, she slowed her pace.

Silly to run, she told herself. No, she corrected herself, stupid. But she hadn't been prepared to see Ty's sister, the one person who knew all the reasons. To have confronted Jess then, when her mind was already so crowded with Ty, would have been disastrous. Steadying, Asher told herself she just needed a little time to prepare. And it had been obvious Jess had been just as stunned as she. At the moment, Asher was too busy calming herself to wonder why.

She wouldn't, couldn't, think about the last time she'd seen Jessica Starbuck—that hot, close Indian summer afternoon. It would be too easy to remember each word spoken in the careless disorder of the hotel room Asher had shared with Ty. She would remember the hurt, the frantic packing, then her irrevocable decision to go to Eric.

Oh, Ty had been right, she had run away—but she hadn't escaped. So little had changed in three years, and so much. Her heart had remained constant. With a sigh Asher admitted it had been foolish to believe she could take back what she had given so long ago. Ty Starbuck was her first lover, and the only man she had ever loved.

A child had been conceived, then lost before it could be born. She'd never forgiven herself for the accident that had taken that precious, fragile life from her. Perhaps more than a lack of love and understanding, it had been the loss of Ty's child that had destroyed any hope for her marriage.

And if the child had lived? she asked herself wearily. What then? Could she have kept it from him? Could she have remained the wife of one man while bearing the child of another? Asher shook her head. No, she would no longer dwell on possibilities. She'd lost Ty, his child, and the support of her own father. There could be no greater punishments to face. She would make her own future.

The touch of a hand on her shoulder had her whirling around. Asher stared up at Ty, her mind a blank, her emotions in turmoil. A hush seemed to spread over the garden, so she could hear the whisper of air over leaves and blossoms. The scent that reached her was sweet and heady—like a first kiss. He said nothing, nor did she until his hand slid down her arm to link with hers.

"Worried about the match?"

Almost afraid he would sense them, Asher struggled to push all thoughts of the past aside. "Concerned," she amended, nearly managing a smile. "Rayski's top seed."

"You've beaten her before."

"And she's beaten me." It didn't occur to her to remove her hand from his or to mask her doubts. Slowly the tension seeped out of her. Through the link of hands Ty felt it. They had stood here before, and the memory was sweet.

"Play her like you played Conway," he advised. "Their styles are basically the same."

With a laugh Asher ran her free hand through her hair. "That's supposed to be a comfort?"

"You're better than she is," he said simply, and earned an astonished stare. Smiling, he brushed his fingers carelessly over her cheek. "More consistent," he explained. "She's faster, but you're stronger. That gives you an advantage on clay even though it isn't your best surface."

At a loss, Asher managed a surprised, "Well."

"You've improved," Ty stated as they began to walk. "Your backhand doesn't have the power it should have, but—"

"It worked pretty well on Conway," Asher interrupted testily.

"Could be better."

"It's perfect," she disagreed, rising to the bait before she caught his grin. Her lips curved before she could stop them. "You always knew how to get a rise out of me. You're playing Kilroy," she went on, "I've never heard of him."

"He's been around only two years. Surprised everyone in Melbourne last season." He slipped an arm around her shoulders in a gesture so familiar, neither of them noticed. "What's that flower?"

Asher glanced down. "Lady's slipper."

"Silly name."

"Cynic."

He shrugged. "I like roses."

"That's because it's the only flower you can identify." Without thinking, she leaned her head on his shoulder. "I remember going in to take a bath one night and finding you'd filled the tub with roses. Dozens of them."

The scent of her hair reminded him of much more. "By the time we got around to clearing them out, it took over an hour."

Her sigh was wistful. "It was wonderful. You could always surprise me by doing something absurd."

"A tub of lady's slippers is absurd," he corrected. "A tub of roses is classy."

Her laughter was quick and appreciative. Her head still rested on his shoulders. "We filled everything in the room that could pass for a vase, including a bottle of ginger ale. Sometimes when I—" She cut herself off, abruptly realizing she would say too much.

"When you what?" Ty demanded as he turned her to face him. When she only shook her head, he tightened his grip. "Would you remember sometimes, in the middle of the night? Would you wake up and hurt because you couldn't forget?"

Truth brought tension to the base of her neck. In

defense, Asher pressed her palms against his chest. "Ty, please."

"I did." He gave her a frustrated shake that knocked her head back. "Oh, God, I did. I've never stopped wanting you. Even hating you I wanted you. Do you know what it's like to be awake at three o'clock in the morning and need someone, and know she's in another man's bed."

"No, no, don't." She was clinging to him, her cheek pressed against his, her eyes tightly shut. "Ty, don't."

"Don't what?" he demanded as he drew her head back. "Don't hate you? Don't want you? Hell, I can't do anything else."

His eyes blazed into her, dark with fury, hot with passion. She could feel the race of his heart compete with hers. Abandoning pride, she pressed her lips to his.

At the instant of contact he stood still, neither giving nor taking. On a moan she drew him closer, letting her lips have their way. A shudder coursed through him, an oath ripped out, then he was responding, demanding, exciting. Why had he tried to resist? Nothing was clear to him as her lips raced crazily over his face. Wasn't this what he wanted? To have her again, to prove he could, to purge his system of her once and for all. Motives dimmed in desire. There was only Asher—the sweet taste of her, her scent more heady, more seductive than the garden of flowers. He couldn't breathe and not fill himself on her. So he surrendered to the persuading lips and soft body that had haunted his dreams.

Dragging his lips from hers only a moment, Ty

pulled her through the fragile branches of a willow. The sun filtered through the curtain of leaves, giving intermittent light. In the cool dimness his mouth sought hers again and found it yielding. The blood pounded in his veins.

He had to know if her body was the same, unchanged during the years he'd been denied her. As his hand took her breast he groaned. She was small and firm and familiar. Through the material of her jacket he felt the nipple harden in quick response. Impatient, he tugged the zipper down, then dove under her shirt until he found the smooth tender flesh that had always made him feel his hands were too rough. Yet she didn't draw away as his calluses met her. She pressed against him. Her moan was not one of discomfort, but of unmistakable pleasure.

Trembling, her fingers reached for his hair. He could feel the urgency in them just as he could taste it on her heated lips. He broke the kiss only to change angles, then deepened it, allowing his tongue to drink up all the dark flavors of her mouth. Against his palm her heart thudded wildly, but only his fingers moved to arouse her.

Slowly his other hand journeyed to her hip to mold the long, slender bone. He was lost somewhere between yesterday and today. The heavy fragrance of flowers still wet with morning dew was more seductive than perfume. Half dreaming, Ty took his mouth to her throat. He heard her sigh float off on the scented air. Was she dreaming too? Was the past overlapping this moment for her as well as for him? The thoughts drifted into his mind, then out again before they could be answered. Nothing mattered but that he was holding her again.

From far off came a ripple of laughter. Ty brought his mouth back to Asher's. A rapid smattering of French drifted to him. Ty drew her closer until their bodies seemed fused. Footsteps and a giggle. Like a dreamer, he sensed the intrusion and swore against it. For another moment he clung, drawing on her lingering passion.

When he released her, Asher was breathless and swaying. Wordlessly he stared down at her with eyes nearly black with emotion. Her lips were parted, swollen from his, and he gave in to need and kissed her one long last time. Gently now, slowly, to store up every dram of sweetness. This time she trembled, her breath coming harsh and fast like a diver's who breaks surface after a long submersion. Disoriented, she gripped his arms.

How long had they been there? she wondered. It could have been seconds or days. All she was sure of was that the longing had intensified almost beyond control. Her blood was racing in her veins, her heart pounding desperately. She was alive. So alive. And no longer certain which path she would take.

"Tonight," Ty murmured, bringing her palm to his lips.

The vibration shot up her arm and into her core. "Ty . . ." Asher shook her head as she tried to draw her hand away. His fingers tightened.

"Tonight," he repeated.

"I can't." Seeing the temper shoot into his eyes, Asher covered their joined hands with her free one. "Ty, I'm frightened."

The quiet admission killed his anger. He let out a weary sigh. "Damn you, Asher."

Saying nothing, she wrapped her arms around his waist, pressing her cheek to his chest. Automatically Ty reached to smooth her hair. His eyes closed. "I'm sorry," she whispered. "I was frightened of you once before. It seems to be happening again." And I love you, she told him silently. As much as ever. More, she realized. More, because of the years of famine.

"Asher." He held her away from him. She felt the passion swirling around him. "I won't promise to wait for you to come to me this time. I won't promise to be gentle and patient. Things aren't the same."

She shook her head, but in agreement. "No, things aren't the same. It might be better, much better for both of us if we just stayed away from each other."

Ty laughed shortly. "We won't."

"If we tried," Asher began.

"*I* won't."

She let out a breath of exasperation. "You're pressuring me."

"Damn right." Before she could decide whether to laugh or to scream, she was in his arms again. "Do you think I don't feel pressured too?" he demanded with a sudden intensity that kept Asher from answering. "Every time I look at you I remember the way things were for us and drive myself crazy trying to figure out why you left me. Do you know what that does to me?"

She gripped his upper arms with strong hands. "You have to understand, I won't go back. Whatever happens to us now begins now. No questions, no whys." She saw the anger boiling in his eyes, but kept hers level. "I mean that, Ty. I can't give you explanations. I won't dig up the past."

"You expect me to live with that?"

"I expect nothing," she said quietly. The tone caused him to look deeper for the answers she refused to give. "And I've agreed to nothing. Not yet."

"You ask for too much," he bit off as he released her. "Too damn much."

She wanted to go to him, go back in his arms and beg him to forget the past. Perhaps it was possible to live for the moment if one wanted to badly enough. It might have been pride that stopped her, or the deeply ingrained survival instinct she had developed since that long-ago September afternoon when she had fled from him and the prospect of pain. Asher laced her fingers together and stared down at them. "Yes, I know. I'm sorry, Ty, we'll only hurt each other."

Tense and tormented, he turned back. "I've never wanted to hurt you, Asher. Not even when I thought I did."

The ache spread so quickly, she almost gasped from it. Isn't that what Jess had said that day? *He'd never want to hurt you . . . never want to hurt you.* Asher could hear the words echoing inside her head. "Neither of us wanted to," she murmured. "Both of us did. Isn't it foolish to do it again?"

"Look at me." The command was quiet and firm. Bracing herself, Asher obeyed. His eyes were locked on hers—those dark, penetrating eyes that conveyed such raw feeling. Gently he touched her cheek.

Without hesitation her hand rose to cover his. "Now," he whispered, "ask me again."

A long, shuddering breath escaped. "Oh, Ty, I was so sure I could prevent this. So sure I could resist you this time."

"And now?"

"Now I'm not sure of anything." She shook her head before he could speak again. "Don't ask now. Give us both some time."

He started to protest, then managed to restrain it. He'd waited three years, a bit longer wouldn't matter. "Some time," he agreed, lowering his hand. But as she started to relax, he took her wrist. The grip was neither gentle nor patient. "The next time, Asher, I won't ask."

She nodded, accepting. "Then we understand each other."

His smile was a trifle grim. "That we do. I'll walk you back." He drew her through the curtain of leaves.

Chapter Five

𝓕ifth set. Seventh game. At the baseline Ty crouched, ready to spring for Michael's serve. The air was heavy, the sky thick with rain-threatening clouds so that the light was dreary. Ty didn't notice. He didn't notice the stadium full of people, some dangling through the railings, some hanging from the scoreboard. He didn't notice the shouts and whistles that were either for or against him.

Tennis was a game of the individual. That was what had drawn him to it. There was no one to blame for a loss, no one to praise for a win but yourself. It was a game of motion and emotion, both of which he excelled in.

He had looked forward to meeting Michael in the semis. The Australian played a hot, passionate game full of dramatic gestures, furious mutters and pizzazz. There were perhaps five competitors Ty fully respected, Michael being one of them. Wanting to win was only a step below wanting a challenge. A fight. He'd grown up scrapping. Now the racket was merely an extension of his arm. The match was a bout. The bout was one on one. It had never—would never—be only a game.

The Australian was a set up, with his momentum still flowing. Ty's only thought at the moment was to break his serve and even the match. Thus far he had spotted no weaknesses in his opponent's game. Like a boxer, he watched for the opening.

He heard the sound of the ball hitting the sweet spot of the racket before it rocketed toward him. It landed deep in the corner of the service court, beautifully placed. Ty's mind and body moved as one as he sprang for the return. Defense, offense, strategy all had to be formulated in a fraction of a second. Strength had to be balanced with form. Both men sprinted over the court for the rally, faces glowing with concentration and sweat. The roar of the crowd rose to meet the distant thunder.

Thus far, the ratio had been nearly ten to one in favor of ground strokes. Ty decided to alter the pacing and go with power. Using a vicious left-to-right slice, he shook Michael's balance. Ty blasted away at the attempted passing shot, barely shortening his backswing. Michael couldn't reach the backhand volley, let alone return it. Love–fifteen.

Shaking the damp hair back from his face, Ty returned to the baseline. A woman in the crowd called out what could have been a congratulations or a proposition. Ty's French wasn't strong enough to decipher the phrase. Michael's serve sent up a puff of smoke. Before his return was over the net, Ty was at mid-court and waiting. A testing ground stroke, a sharp return. A tricky topspin, a slice. Michael's decision to try to lob over Ty was a mistake. The smoking smash careened off the court and into the grandstands. Love–thirty.

Michael walked a complete circle, cursing himself before he took his position again. Casting off impatience, Ty waited. Crouched, swaying side to side, unblinking, he was ready. Both players exploited angles and depths with ground strokes. There was a long, patient rally as each watched for the chance to smash a winner. It might have been pure showmanship if it hadn't been for the sounds of exertion coming from the two players.

A UPI photographer had his motor drive humming as he recorded the game. He framed Ty, arms extended for balance, legs spread for the stretch, face fierce. It crossed his mind as he continued to snap that he wouldn't want to face that American on any playing field.

Gracefully, with an elegance belied by his expression, Ty executed a backhand with a touch of underspin. Michael's return thudded against the net. Love–forty.

Angry and shaken, Michael punched his first serve into the net. Having no choice at game point, he placed his next serve carefully. Ty went straight for the volley and took the net. The exchange was fast and furious, the players moving on instinct, the crowd screaming in a mixture of languages. Ty's wrist was locked. The ball whipped from racket to racket at terrifying speed. There were bare seconds between contact, making both men anticipate flight rather than see it. Changing tactics in the wink of an instant, Ty brought the racket face under at the moment of impact. With a flick of a wrist he dropped a dump shot over the net. Risky, experts would say. Gutsy, fans would claim. Ty would ignore both. Game and set.

"Oh, Mac!" Jess leaned back and expelled a long breath. "I'd nearly forgotten what it was like to watch Ty play."

"You watched him just a few weeks ago," he pointed out, using a damp handkerchief to wipe his neck. The wish for his air-conditioned office flitted only briefly into his mind.

"On television," Jess returned. "That's different. Being here . . . can't you feel it?"

"I thought it was the humidity."

Laughing, Jess shook her head. "Always down to earth, Mac, that's why I love you."

Her smile seemed to open just for him. It could still make his blood sing. "Then I intend to stay there," he murmured, kissing her knuckles. Feeling her hand tense, he looked up, puzzled. Her eyes were aimed over his shoulder. Curious, he turned, spotting a few tennis faces he recognized. Among them was Asher Wolfe. It was on her that his wife's gaze was locked.

"That's the former Lady Wickerton, isn't it?" he asked casually. "She's stunning."

"Yes." Jess tore her eyes away, but the tension in her fingers remained. "Yes, she is."

"She won her match this morning. We'll have an American going into the women's finals." Jess said nothing as Mac stuffed the handkerchief back into his pocket. "She was away from the game for a while, wasn't she?"

"Yes."

Intrigued by his wife's flat answer, Mac probed. "Didn't she and Ty have something going a few years back?"

"It was nothing." With a nervous swallow Jess prayed she spoke the truth. "Just a passing thing. She's not Ty's type. Asher's very cool, much more suited to Wickerton than to Ty. He was attracted to that for a while, that's all." She moistened her lips. "And it was obvious she wasn't serious about him, otherwise she'd never have married Wickerton so quickly. She was making Ty unhappy, very unhappy."

"I see," Mac murmured after a moment. Jess had spoken too quickly and too defensively. Studying his wife's profile, he wondered. "I suppose Ty's too involved in his career to be serious about a woman?"

"Yes." The look Jess gave him was almost pleading. "Yes, he'd never have let her go if he'd been in love with her. Ty's too possessive."

"And proud," he reminded her quietly. "I don't think he'd run after any woman, no matter how he felt about her."

Feeling her stomach roll, Jess said nothing. She turned to watch her brother take the position for his first serve.

Instead of the hazy afternoon she saw a brilliant morning. Instead of the clay of Roland Garros she saw the nearly empty grass courts of Forest Hills. Ty was leaning over the rail, staring out at center court.

She had a fanciful thought that he looked like the captain of a ship with his eyes on the open, endless sea. In her world she loved no one more than him, could conceive of loving no one more. He was brother and father and hero. He'd provided her with a home, clothes and an education, asking nothing in return. As a result, she would have given him anything.

Crossing to him, she slipped her arm around him, nestling her head in the crook of his shoulder.

"Thinking about this afternoon?" she murmured. He was slated to face Chuck Prince in the finals of the U.S. Open.

"Hmm?" Distracted, Ty shrugged. "No, not really."

"It must feel odd to compete against your closest friend."

"You just forget you're friends for a couple hours," Ty returned.

He was brooding; she sensed it. And unhappy. There was no one, including her mother, Jess felt more loyalty to. Her grip around him tightened. "Ty, what is it?"

"Just restless."

"Have you fought with Asher?"

Absently he tousled her hair. "No, I haven't fought with Asher."

He lapsed into silence for so long that Jess began to suspect he wasn't telling the entire truth. She was already worried about him and Asher. The relationship had lasted longer than was habitual for Ty. Jess saw Asher's reserve as coldness, her independence as indifference. She didn't hang on Ty as other women did. She didn't listen raptly to every word he spoke. She didn't adore him.

"Do you ever think back, Jess?" he asked suddenly.

"Think back?"

"To when we were kids." His eyes skimmed over the manicured courts, but didn't see them. "That crummy apartment with the paper walls. The De-Marcos next door screaming at each other in the middle of the night. The stairwell always smelled of old garbage and stale sweat."

The tone of his voice disturbed her. Seeking comfort as much as to comfort, she turned her face into his chest. "Not often. I guess I don't remember it as well as you. I hadn't turned fifteen when you got us out."

"I wonder sometimes if you can ever escape that, if you can ever really turn your back on it." His eyes were focused on something Jess couldn't see. She strained to share the vision. "Old garbage and stale sweat," he repeated quietly. "I can't forget that. I asked Asher once what smell she remembered most from her childhood. She said the wisteria that hung over her bedroom window."

"Ty, I don't understand."

He swore softly. "Neither do I."

"You left all that behind," she began.

"I left it," he corrected her. "That doesn't mean I left it behind. We were having dinner last night. Wickerton stopped by the table and started a conversation about French Impressionists. After five minutes I didn't know what the hell they were talking about."

Jess bristled. She knew because Ty had sent her to college. She knew because he had provided the opportunity. "You should have told him to get lost."

With a laugh Ty kissed her cheek. "That was my first thought." Abruptly he sobered. "Then I watched them. They understand each other, speak the same language. It made me realize there are some fences you just can't climb."

"You could if you wanted to."

"Maybe. I don't." He let out a long breath. "I don't really give a damn about French Impressionists. I don't give a damn about the mutual friends they have that are distant cousins of the Queen of England, or who won at Ascot last month." Storm warnings were in his eyes, but he shrugged. "Even if I did, I wouldn't fit into that kind of life because I'd always remember the garbage and sweat."

"Asher has no business encouraging that man," Jess stated heatedly. "He's been following her around since Paris."

Ty gave a grim laugh. "She doesn't encourage or discourage. Drawing room conversation," he murmured. "Ingrained manners. She's different from us, Jess, I've known that all along."

"If *she'd* tell him to get lost—"

"She couldn't tell anyone to get lost any more than she could sprout wings and fly."

"She's cold."

"She's different," Ty returned immediately but without heat. He cupped his sister's chin in his hand. "You and me, we're the same. Everything's up front. If we want to shout, we shout. If we want to throw something, we throw it. Some people can't."

"Then they're stupid."

This time his laugh was warm and genuine. "I love you, Jess."

Throwing her arms around him, she hugged him fiercely. "I can't bear to see you unhappy. Why do you let her do this to you?"

Frowning, Ty stroked her hair. "I've been trying to figure that out. Maybe . . . maybe I just need a shove in the right direction."

Jess held him tighter, searching her mind for the answer.

Seventh set. Tenth game. The crowd was as vocal, as enthusiastic and as hungry as it had been an hour before. Leaning forward in his seat, his eyes glued to the ball, Chuck sat between Asher and Madge.

"You've got something riding on this one, don't you, cowboy?" Madge commented dryly though her own heart was pumping. Chuck would face the winner in the finals.

"It's the best match I've seen in two years." His own face was damp, his own muscles tense. The ball traveled at such speeds, it was often only a white blur.

Asher spoke to neither of them. Her objectivity had been long since destroyed. Ty enthralled her. Both men possessed the raw athletic ability competitors admired and envied. Both were draining the other's resources without mercy. But it was Ty, always Ty, who ripped the emotion from her.

She could admire Michael, admit his brilliance,

but he didn't cause that slow, churning ache in her stomach. Had she not once been Ty's lover, had she not even known him, would she still be so drawn? Controlled rage. How was it a woman raised in such an ordered, sheltered existence would be pulled irresistibly to a man with such turbulent passion? Opposites attract? she wondered. No, that was much too simple.

Sitting in the crowded stadium, Asher felt the thrill of desire as clearly as though she had been naked in his arms. She felt no shame. It was natural. She felt no fear. It was inevitable. Years made up of long, unending days vanished. What a waste of time, she thought suddenly. No, a loss, she corrected herself. A loss of time—nothing's ever wasted. *Tonight.* The decision came to her as effortlessly as it had the first time. Tonight they would be together. And if it was only once—if once was all he wanted— it would have to be enough. The long wait was over. She laughed out loud in relief and joy. Chuck sent her an odd look.

"He's going to win," Asher said on a second laugh. Leaning on the rail, she rested her chin on her folded hands. "Oh, yes, he's going to win."

There was a dull ache in his racket arm that Ty ignored. The muscles in his legs promised to cramp the moment he stopped moving. He wouldn't give in to them any more than he would give in to the man across the net. One thing hadn't changed in twenty years. He still hated to lose.

A point away from the match, he played no less tigerishly than he had in the first game. The rallies had been long and punishing. The ball whistled.

Sweat dripped. For the last twenty minutes Ty had forsaken artistry for cunning. It was working.

Power for power, they were in a dead heat, so that Ty chose to outmaneuver the Australian. He worked him over the court, pacing him, some might say stalking him. The game went to deuce three times while the crowd grew frantic. An ace gave him advantage—a screeching bullet that brought Ty the final impetus he needed. Then Ty played him hot-bloodedly. The men drove from side to side, their faces masks of effort and fury. The shot came that he'd been waiting for. Michael's awesome backhand drove crosscourt to his southpaw forehand. The ball came to Ty at waist level. Michael didn't even have to see the return to know it was over.

Game, set and match.

The heat hit him then, and the fatigue. It took an effort not to stagger. Simply to have fallen to his knees would have been a relief. He walked to the net.

Michael took his hand, then draped his free arm around Ty's shoulder. "Damn you, Starbuck," he managed breathlessly. "You nearly killed me."

Ty laughed, using his opponent for balance a moment. "You too."

"I need a bloody drink." Michael straightened, giving Ty a glazed grin. "Let's go get drunk."

"You're on."

Turning, they separated, victor and vanquished, to face the press, the showers and the massage tables. Ty grabbed the towel someone handed him, nodding at the questions and congratulations being hurled at him. Behind the cloth he could hear the click and whirl of cameras. He was too weary to curse them. Someone was gathering his rackets. He could hear the clatter of wood on wood. The strength that had flowed freely through him only moments before drained. Exhausted, he let the drenched towel fall. His eyes met Asher's.

So blue, he thought. Her eyes are so blue. And cool, and deep. He could drown in them blissfully. The unbearable heat vanished, as though someone had opened a window to a fresh spring breeze.

"Congratulations." When she smiled, his fatigue slid away. Strangely it wasn't desire that replaced it, but comfort, sweet simple comfort.

"Thanks." He took the racket bag from her. Their hands barely brushed.

"I suppose the press is waiting for you inside."

The short retort Ty made was both agreement and opinion. On a low laugh she stepped closer.

"Can I buy you dinner?"

The quirk of his brow was the only indication of surprise. "Sure."

"I'll meet you at seven in the lobby of the hotel."

"All right."

"Starbuck, what do you feel was the turning point of the match?"

"What strategy will you use playing Prince in the finals?"

Ty didn't answer the reporters, didn't even hear them as he watched Asher weave her way through the crowd. From overhead Jess watched with a small, fluttering sensation of déjà vu.

Ty got under the stream of the shower fully

dressed. He let the cool water sluice over him while he stripped. A reporter from *World of Sports* leaned against a tiled wall, scribbling notes and tossing questions. Naked, with his clothes in a soggy heap at his feet, Ty answered. Always, he handled the press naturally because he didn't give a damn what they printed. He knew his mother kept a scrapbook, but he never read the articles or interviews. Lathering the soap over his face with both hands, he washed the sticky sweat away. Someone passed him a plastic jug of fruit juice. With the water streaming over him, he guzzled it down, replacing lost fluid. The weakness was seeping back, and with it the pain. He made his way to the massage table by instinct, then collapsed onto it.

Strong fingers began to work on him. Questions still hammered in his ears, but now he ignored them. Ty simply closed his eyes and shut them out. A line of pain ran up his calf as the muscles were kneaded. He winced and held on, knowing relief would follow. For ten agonizing minutes he lay still while his body was rubbed and pounded. He began to drift. Like a mother's memory of the pain of childbirth, his memory of the pain began to dim. He could remember winning. And he could remember dark blue eyes. With those two visions tangling in his mind, he slept.

The floor of the lobby was marble. White marble veined with pink. Madge had commented that it would be the devil to keep clean. Her husband had dryly commented that she wouldn't know one end of the mop from the other. Asher sat, listening to their comfortable banter while she told herself she wasn't nervous. It was six-fifty.

She'd dressed carefully, choosing a simple crêpe de Chine as pale as the inside of a peach. Her hair fluffed back from her face, exposing the tiny pearl and coral drops at her ears. Her ringless fingers were interlaced.

"Where are you eating?"

Asher brought her attention back to Madge. "A little place on the Left Bank." There was an enthusiastic violinist, she remembered. Ty had once passed him twenty American dollars and cheerfully told him to get lost.

At the bellow of thunder Madge glanced toward the lobby doors. "You're going to play hell getting a cab tonight." She leaned back. "Have you seen Ty since the match?"

"No."

"Chuck said both he and Michael were sleeping on the tables like babies." A chuckle escaped as she crossed strong, short legs. "Some industrious stringer for a French paper got a couple of classic shots."

"Athletes in repose," her husband mused.

"It kind of blows the tough-guy image."

Asher smiled, thinking how young and vulnerable Ty looked in sleep. When the lids closed over those dramatic eyes, he reminded her of an exhausted little boy. It was the only time the frenetic energy stilled. Something stirred in her. If the child had lived . . . Hurriedly she censored the thought.

"Hey, isn't that Ty's sister?"

Asher turned her head to see Jess and Mac crossing the lobby. "Yes." Their eyes met, leaving no choice. Gripping her husband's hand, Jess walked across the white marble.

"Hello, Asher."

"Jess."

A quick moistening of lips betrayed nerves. "I don't think you know my husband. Mackenzie Derick, Lady Wickerton."

"Asher Wolfe," she replied smoothly, taking Mac's hand. "Are you related to Martin?"

"My uncle," Mac informed her. "Do you know him?"

The smile brought warmth to her eyes. "Very well." She made the rest of the introductions with a natural poise Mac approved of. Cool, yes, he mused, remembering his wife's description. But with an underlying vibrancy perhaps a man would discern more quickly than another woman. He began to wonder if Jess's opinion of Ty's feelings was accurate.

"Are you a tennis fan, Mr. Derick?" Asher asked him.

"Mac," he supplied. "Only by marriage. And no, I don't play, much to Uncle Martin's disgust."

Asher laughed, appreciating the humor in his eyes. A strong man, she thought instantly. His own man. He wouldn't take second place to Ty in his wife's life. "Martin should be satisfied having cultivated one champion." Her eyes drifted to Jess, who was sitting straight and tense beside Madge. "Is your mother well?"

"Yes, yes, Mom's fine." Though she met the cool, clear gaze, her fingers began to pleat the material of her skirt. "She's at home with Pete."

"Pete?"

"Our son."

Asher's throat constricted. Mac noticed with some surprise that her knuckles whitened briefly on the arm of her chair. "I didn't know you'd had a baby. Ada must be thrilled to have a grandchild." The pressure on her heart was unbearable. Her smile was casual. "How old is he?" she made herself ask.

"Fourteen months." As the tension built in one woman, it flowed out of the other. Jess was already reaching into her purse for her wallet. "I swear he never walked, he started out running. Mom says he's like Ty. He has his coloring too." She was offering a picture. Asher had no choice but to accept it.

There was some of his father in him—the shape of the face. But the Starbuck genes were strong. The baby's hair was dark and thick, like his mother's. Like Ty's. The eyes were large and gray. Asher wondered if she could actually feel the air of perpetual motion around the child, or if she imagined it. Another baby would have had dark hair and gray eyes. Hadn't she pictured the face countless times?

"He's beautiful," she heard herself say in a calm voice. "You must be very proud of him." When she handed the snapshot back her hands were perfectly steady.

"Jess thinks he should wait until he's twelve before he runs for president."

Asher smiled, but this time Mac didn't find the

reflected warmth in her eyes. "Has Ty bought him a racket yet?"

"You know him very well," Mac observed.

"Yes." She looked back at Jess steadily. "Tennis and his family come first, always."

"I hate to admit it," Madge put in with a sigh, "but I can remember a dozen years ago when this one was a skinny teenager, chewing her fingernails at every one of Ty's matches. Now you're a mother."

Jess grinned, holding out her hands for inspection. "And I still bite my nails at Ty's matches."

It was Asher who saw him first. But then, her senses were tuned for him. Ty stepped off the elevator dressed in slim black slacks and a smoke-gray shirt. He wouldn't have chosen the shirt because it matched his eyes so perfectly. Asher knew he wore it because it would have been the first thing his hand had grabbed from the closet. He wore clothes with the casual style of one who gave no thought to them and still looked marvelous. A disciplined body and trained grace made it inevitable. His hair had been combed, but defied order. He paused briefly, even in stillness communicating motion. Asher's heartbeat was a dull, quick thud.

"Oh, there's Ty!" Jess sprang up, hurrying across the lobby to meet him. "I didn't get to congratulate you. You were absolutely wonderful."

Though his arm slipped around her, Jess saw that his eyes had drifted over her head. Without turning, she knew who they focused on.

Asher didn't rise, nor did she speak.

"Well, Starbuck, you earned your pay today,"

Madge commented. "The Dean and I are going to the Lido to hold Michael's hand."

"Tell him I lost three pounds on the court today." He spoke to her, lightly enough, but his eyes never left Asher's.

"I don't think that's going to make him feel a hell of a lot better," she returned, giving her husband a nudge as she rose. "Well, we're off to fight for a taxi. Anyone going our way?"

"As a matter of fact," Mac began, picking up the hint easily, "Jess and I were on our way out too."

"Want a lift, Ty?" Madge's husband gave her an offended look as she ground her heel into his foot. But he shut his mouth firmly when Madge shot him a deadly glance.

Even to a man who rarely comprehended subtleties, it became obvious there were things being said without words. The little group had simply ceased to exist for Ty and Asher. After a hard look at the silent couple The Dean straightened his glasses and grinned at his wife.

"I guess not, huh?"

"You're so quick, babe." Madge began shepherding the rest toward the doors. "Anyone know some French obscenities? It's the best way to get a cab in the rain."

Asher rose slowly. From behind her she could hear the ding of a bell on the desk and the whoosh of the storm as the doors were opened then quickly closed. For a moment Ty thought she looked like something that should be enclosed in glass. Not to be touched, not to be soiled. She reached out her hand.

When he took it, it was warm. Flesh and blood.

In unspoken agreement they turned away from the doors and walked to the elevator.

Chapter Six

They didn't speak, but then they didn't need to. With one hand still holding hers, Ty pushed the button for his floor. The elevator began its silent rise. Once, the hand in his trembled lightly. He found it unbearably exciting. The numbers above their heads flashed ponderously until at last the car stopped. When the doors slid open they stepped into the carpeted hall together.

Asher heard the key jingle against loose change as Ty reached into his pocket. She heard the click of the lock before he released her hand. The choice was still hers. She stepped out of the light into the dimness of his room.

It smelled of him. That was her first thought. The air carried Ty's lingering fragrance. Something sharp, something vital. Something she had never forgotten. All at once her nerves began to jump.

The poise that had carried her this far fell away. Searching for something to say, she wandered the room. It was untidy, with a shirt thrown here, shoes tossed there. She knew if she opened the closet, she would find a neat stack of rackets, the only semblance of order. Instead, she moved to the window. Rain ran like tears down the glass.

"It's going to storm all night."

As if to accent her words, lightning split the sky. Asher counted to five, then heard the thunder answer. Hundreds of lights spread through the darkness. The city was there, crowded, moving—distant. Staring through the wet glass, she waited for Ty to speak.

Silence. The patter of rain on the window. The distant hum of traffic. Another moan of thunder. Unable to bear it, Asher turned.

He was watching her. The small bedside lamp threw both light and shadow into the room. His stance was neither relaxed nor threatening, and she understood. He had given her a choice before she entered. Now he wouldn't let her go. A bridge had been burned. Asher felt nothing but relief that the decision was already made. But her fingers were numb as she reached to loosen the thin belt at her waist.

Crossing to her, Ty laid his hands over hers, stopping the movement. Asher stared up at him, unsure, as nervous as the first time. Without speaking he took her face in his hands to study her. He wanted to remember her this way—in shadowed light with the fury of a storm at her back. Her eyes were dark with traces of fear, traces of desire. In a gesture of surrender her arms had dropped to her sides. But he didn't want surrender—perhaps she had forgotten.

As he lowered his head Ty watched her lids shut, her lips part in anticipation. Gently he kissed her temple, then the other, then the delicate curve of an eyebrow. Without haste, his eyes closed. He reacquainted himself with her face through taste and touch. Her lips beckoned, but he nibbled along the line of her jaw, on the hollow of her cheek.

His thumb brushed her bottom lip as he whispered kisses over her face. He remembered every curve. Her breath shuddered out as he kissed the corners of her mouth. He brushed his over it, retreating when Asher sought more pressure. There was only the fleeting promise of more. With a moan she gripped his forearms. He'd waited for the strength. He'd waited for the demands. Again he touched his lips to hers, allowing his tongue a brief taste. Now her arms wrapped possessively around him. Now passion exploded, mouth against mouth. Lightning flashed, illuminating them as one form in the ageless wonder of lovers.

"Undress me," she whispered breathlessly, hardly able to speak as her lips fused again and again with his. "I want you to undress me."

In answer, he lowered the zipper slowly, allowing his fingers to trail along her bare skin. He found more silk, something thin and fragile. The dress slithered down her body to lie at her feet. Growing impatient, Asher worked her hands between them to deal with the buttons of his shirt while her mouth continued to cling to his. She felt the hard muscle, the line of ribs, the mat of hair. A moan wrenched from her out of deep, desperate need.

The thigh-length chemise was too much of a barrier. Longing for the intimacy of flesh against flesh, Asher reached to draw down the strap. Again Ty stopped her.

"Don't rush," he murmured, then tore at her control with a deep, lingering kiss. The pressure was hard and demanding, the lips soft and heated. "Come to bed."

In a haze she let him lead her, felt the mattress give under her weight, then his. Anticipation shivered along her skin. "The light," she whispered.

As he circled her throat with his hand, Ty's eyes met hers. "I need to see you." Thunder exploded as his mouth crushed down on hers.

When she would have hurried, he set the pace. Languorous, sleepy, enervating. It seemed her lips alone would pleasure him enough for a lifetime. She was so soft, so moist. Far from pliant, Asher moved against him, inviting, insisting. Her urgency excited him, but Ty chose to savor. Over the silk his hands roamed to trace her shape from thigh to breast. The peaks strained against the sheer material.

He took his mouth to her shoulder, catching the narrow strap of the silk with his teeth. Inch by inch he lowered it until her flesh was exposed to him. She was firm and creamy-white in contrast to the tan of her arms and shoulders.

"So lovely," he whispered while his fingertip brought down the second strap.

When she was naked to the waist, his mouth ranged down slowly, though with her hands in his hair she urged him on. With lips parted, Ty sought the peak of her breast. Asher arched, pressing him down. She wanted him to be greedy, wanted to feel the rough scrape of his tongue. When she did she could no longer be still. Her body vibrated with the beat of a hundred tiny pulses. Desire, raw and primitive, tore through her with the power to obliterate all but one thought. She was woman; he was man. Seeking pleasure, Asher moved under him, letting her hands roam.

He abandoned gentleness because she wanted none. It had always driven him wild when her passion was unleashed. She had no inhibitions, no shame. When they came together like this she was all fire, and as dangerous as the lightning in the night sky. Ty wasn't even aware of his control slipping away. Hard-palmed hands ran bruisingly over tender skin. Short, manicured nails dug into strong shoulders.

His breathing was ragged when he tore the garment from her. She gave him no time to view her nakedness. Her fingers were busy, struggling to remove the last barrier of his clothing. Their frantic movements took them over the bed, tangling in the sheets. Her skin was damp and trembling, but her hands were so strong, and so certain. There could be no more waiting.

A pain stabbed into him as he entered her. It was sharp, then sweet. He thought he heard her cry out as she had that first night when he had taken her innocence. Then she was wrapped around him—

legs, arms. Her mouth fastened on his. The storm crashed directly overhead. They rose with it.

His hand lay lightly on her breast. Asher sighed. Had she ever known such pure contentment? she wondered. No, not even when they had been together before. Then she hadn't known what it would be like to do without him. She shuddered, then moved closer.

"Cold?" Ty drew her to him until her head rested on the curve of his shoulder.

"A little. Where's my chemise?"

"Devoured."

She laughed, flinging her arm around him as though she would never let go. Free, she thought. How wonderful to be free—to love, to laugh. Supporting herself on his chest, she stared down into his face. For once his eyes were calm. A faint smile curved his lips. Beneath her his breathing was even and slow, to match hers. To match, her mind repeated. They had always been like two halves of the same whole.

"Oh, God, I missed you, Ty." On those words she buried her face against his throat. Empty, empty, she thought. It seemed like a lifetime of emptiness had been wiped away with an hour of fulfillment.

"Asher—"

"No, no questions. No questions." Wildly she rained kisses over his face. "Just feel, just be with me. I need to laugh tonight, the way we used to."

He stopped her hurried movements by taking her head in his hands. There was a plea in her eyes and a light trace of desperation. No, he didn't want to see that now. Pushing away the questions that drummed in his head, he smiled at her.

"I thought you were going to buy me dinner."

Relief washed over her before she grinned. "I have no idea what you're talking about."

"You asked me for a date."

Tossing her head back, she arched an elegant brow. "*I* asked you? You've been out in the heat too long, Starbuck."

"Dinner," he repeated, rolling her over until he loomed above her.

"As far as I can tell, you've already eaten a sixty-dollar silk chemise. Are you still hungry?"

For an answer, he lowered his mouth to her neck and bit, none too gently. Laughing, she tried to twist away. "Food," he muttered. "I have to eat."

Remembering a weakness, she found the spot on his ribs and squeezed. His body jerked, giving her the opportunity to slither away. She was giggling like a girl when he grabbed her and pulled her back. "How many people know the indomitable Starbuck is ticklish?" she demanded when he pinned her arms over her head. "What would the press pay to find out?"

"About the same as they'd pay to find out the elegant Asher Wolfe has a heart-shaped birthmark on her very attractive bottom."

Asher considered this a moment. "Even," she decided. Her smile slanted seductively. "Do you really want to go out to eat?"

Desire fluttered lightly in the pit of his stomach as he looked down on her. The light angled across her face, accenting the smooth, glowing skin and darkened eyes. The thunder was a distant rumble now, but he felt it vibrate in his head.

"There's always room service," he murmured, tasting her lips. He kept her arms pinned as he dropped light, teasing kisses over her face. Nestling in the vulnerable curve of her neck, he used his tongue to stir and arouse.

"Ty," she moaned, unable to struggle against the captivity. "Make love to me."

His chuckle was low and he was pleased. "Oh, I am. This time," he whispered into her ear, "we won't hurry. Hours, love." His tongue darted to her ear, making her squirm in agonized delight. "Hours and hours." Then he shifted, bringing her close to his side. Cradling her, he felt her heart pounding against him. When he reached for the phone, Asher glanced up, puzzled. "Food," he reminded her.

She gave a weak laugh. "I should have remembered your stomach comes first."

His hand grazed over her breast. "Not necessarily." Her nipple was already taut. He flicked his thumb over it lazily.

"Ty—" With a kiss he silenced her.

"Champagne," he said into the phone while driving Asher mad with careless strokes and fondling. "Dom Pérignon. Caviar," he went on, sending her a questioning look that she was powerless to answer. "Beluga." He gave her a light kiss, running his hand down to the flat of her stomach. She quivered, turning into him. Legs tangled as he brushed his lips over her shoulder. "Cold shrimp." He bit her tender bottom lip. "Mmm, that'll do. Yes, for two." As he dropped the phone back on its cradle, Asher found his mouth in a desperate, yearning kiss. "Food excites you?" he mumbled against the hungry lips. Struggling not to take her instantly, he ran his hand to her hip, kneading warm flesh.

"I want you." Her voice was low and throaty, her hands questing. "I want you now."

"Shh." Slow, patient, his stroking aroused rather than subdued. "Relax. There's time. I want to see you again." He drew away from her. "Really see you."

She was burning for him. Now she lay naked and vulnerable under his gaze. As she watched, his eyes darkened, grew stormy. Her breathing quickened. When she reached out he took her hand, burying his lips in the palm.

"You're more beautiful than ever," he said huskily. "It shouldn't be possible. I've looked at you so many times and have been afraid to touch."

"No." Asher pulled him to her until they were heart to heart. "I'm never more alive than when you touch me." With a sigh Ty nestled down until his head rested between her breasts. Asher combed her fingers through his hair as contentment layered over desire. "Today, when I watched you playing Michael, I wanted you. Sitting there, surrounded by thousands of people in the middle of the afternoon, all I could think about was being with you like this." She gave a gurgle of laughter. "Wicked thoughts, such wonderfully wicked thoughts."

"So your invitation to dinner carried an ulterior motive."

"In your weakened condition I knew you'd be a

pushover, though I had thought I'd have to take you out and ply you with food and wine first."

"And if I'd refused?"

"I'd have come up with something else."

Grinning, he lifted his head. "What?"

Asher shrugged. "I could have come up here and seduced you before you'd gotten your strength back."

"Hmm . . . I almost wish I'd said no."

"Too late. I have you now."

"I could get stubborn."

Slowly she smiled. "I know your weaknesses," she whispered, running a fingertip up the nape of his neck. His shudder was quick and uncontrollable. Leaning up, she took his face in her hands. Lazily she rubbed her lips over his, then deepened the touch into a kiss—a long, draining taste that left him weak. Her tongue glided over his, then retreated.

"Asher." On an oath he crushed her beneath him, savaging her mouth with a need that had risen so quickly, it left him dazed. He didn't hear the discreet knock on the door, nor did he understand her murmurs.

"The door," she managed. "Ty, it's room service."

"What?"

"The door."

Laying his forehead on hers, he struggled to recapture his control. "They're awful damn quick," he muttered. He found he was trembling. How could he have forgotten that she could make him tremble? After letting out a long breath, he rose. Asher pulled the sheets up to her chin and watched him cross to the closet.

A beautiful body, she thought, both proud and admiring. Long and lean, with a network of muscle. She looked her fill as he rummaged through his closet for a robe. Strong shoulders, trim waist, narrow hips and long legs. An athlete's body, or a dancer's. He was made to compete.

He shrugged into the robe, belting it carelessly. Grinning, he turned to her. Asher's heart lodged in her throat. "Ty, you're so beautiful."

His eyes widened in astonishment. Torn between amusement and masculine discomfort, he headed for the door. "Good God," he said, making Asher smother a giggle. She brought her knees up to her chest as he signed the check at the door. In some ways, she mused, he was a little boy. To his way of thinking, the word *beautiful* applied only to a woman—or to an ace. He'd be more insulted than complimented having it applied to himself. Yet she saw him that way—not only physically. He was a man capable of lovely gestures, a man unashamed of his deep love for his mother, unafraid to show tenderness. He had no cruelty in him, though on the court he was unmerciful. His temper was explosive, but he was incapable of holding a grudge. Asher realized that it was his basic capacity for feeling that she had missed most of all. And still he had never, in all their closeness, in all the months of intimacy, told her that he loved her. If he had once said the words, she would never have left him.

"Where have you gone?"

Asher turned her head to see him standing beside a tray, a bottle of champagne in his hands. Quickly she shook her head and smiled again. "Nowhere." She cocked her head at the bottle. "All that just for us?"

He walked to the bed and sat on the edge. "Did you want some too?" The cork came off with a resounding pop as she cuffed his shoulder. With an easy stretch he rolled the tray toward them. "Here, hold the glasses." Without ceremony he poured champagne until it nearly ran over the rims.

"Ty, it'll spill on the bed."

"Better be careful then," he advised as he set the bottle back in the ice. He grinned as she sat cross-legged, balancing two glasses in her hands. The sheet was held in place over her breasts by arms pressed tight to her sides.

She returned the grin with a glance of exasperation. "Aren't you going to take one?"

"Oh, I don't know." Hooking a finger under the sheet, he nudged it downward, exposing creamy flesh.

"Ty, cut it out, I'll spill it!"

"Better not, we have to sleep here." He urged the sheet a trifle lower. Frustrated, Asher looked from glass to glass. Wine swayed dangerously.

"This is a dirty trick, Starbuck."

"Yeah, I like it."

Asher narrowed her eyes. "I'm going to pour both glasses into your lap."

"Terrible waste," he decided, kissing her. "It's good stuff. I always found it strange," he began, lazily kissing her face as he spoke, "that I was bred for beer and you were bred for champagne, but you haven't any head for it."

"I have a perfectly good head for champagne."

Chuckling, he brushed his lips over her throat. "I remember one very memorable night when we shared a bottle. Three glasses make you crazy. I like you crazy."

"That's absurd." The lift of brow challenged him. Without hesitation Asher brought a glass to her lips, losing the sheet as she drank it. Ty watched the linen pool into her lap before she drained the last drop. "That's one," Asher announced, lifting the second glass. Ty plucked it from her fingers.

"Let's spread it out a little," he advised, amused. He drank, more conservatively, then reached for the tray of caviar. "You like this stuff."

"Mmm." Suddenly hungry, Asher spread a generous amount on a toast point. Ty settled down to the bowl of cold shrimp and spicy sauce. "Here, it's good." Though he allowed her to feed him a bite, he wrinkled his nose.

"Overrated," he stated. "This is better." He popped a shrimp into Asher's mouth.

"'S wonderful," she agreed with a full mouth, then chose another. "I didn't know I was so hungry."

Ty filled her glass again. Could anyone else imagine her, he wondered, sitting naked in bed, licking sauce from her finger? Did anyone else know how totally open she could be? She was talking now, in fits and starts as she ate, replaying her match. Ty let her ramble, pleased just to hear her voice, to see her animation. She was satisfied with her serve, worried about her backhand volley.

Publicly she chose her words with care, and made certain there were few of them. If a reporter could see her now, Ty mused, he'd wear a pencil down to the nub. She was full of joy and doubt, fear and self-congratulation. Words tumbled out without discretion. Her face was animated, her hands gestured. By the time she had slowed down, her second glass was empty. Perhaps she was completely happy, because she wasn't even aware of the sensation. She was simply at ease, completely herself. Comfortably full, she toyed with the last of the caviar.

"Are you worried about playing Chuck in the finals?"

Ty bit into a shrimp. "Why?"

"He was always good," Asher began, frowning a bit. "But he's developed over the past few years."

Grinning, Ty tilted more wine into her glass. "Don't you think I can beat him?"

She sent him a long, considering look. "You were always good too."

"Thanks." After setting the caviar on the tray, he stretched lengthwise on the bed.

"Chuck plays a bit like my father did," Asher mused. "Very clean, very precise. His talent's polished rather than raw."

"Like mine."

"Yes. That raw athletic ability is something every competitor envies. My father used to say that you had more natural talent than any player he'd seen in his career." Over the rim of her glass she smiled down at him. "Yet he always wanted to smooth out your form. Then there were your . . . antics on the court."

Ty laughed, kissing her knee through the sheet. "It used to drive him crazy."

"I imagine he'd be more pleased if he saw you play now."

"And you?" Ty countered. "How would he feel if he saw you play now?"

Asher shifted her eyes from his to stare into her glass. "He won't."

"Why?"

As if to erase the question, she lifted her hand. "Ty, please."

"Asher," he said quietly, grasping her fingers. "You're hurting."

If she could have held it back, she would have. But the words tumbled out. "I let him down. He won't forgive me."

"He's your father."

"And he was my coach."

Unable to comprehend, Ty shook his head. "What difference does that make?"

"All the difference." The pain slipped out. As if to numb it, she swallowed more wine. "Please, not tonight. I don't want anything to spoil tonight."

Her fingers had tightened on his. One by one Ty kissed them until he felt the tension relax. "Nothing could." Over their joined hands, dark, intense eyes met hers. Spontaneously her pulse began to race. "I never got you completely out of my mind," he confessed. "Too many things reminded me—a phrase, a song. Silence. There were times alone at night I would have sworn I heard you breathing in the quiet beside me."

The words moved her . . . hurt her. "Ty, those were yesterdays. We can start now."

"Now," he agreed. "But we'll have to deal with yesterday sooner or later."

Though she opened her mouth to disagree, she knew. "Later then. Right now I don't want to think about anything but being with you."

He grinned, brushing a stray curl from her cheek. "It's difficult to argue with that."

"Don't get cocky," she told him, then tossed off the rest of her champagne. "That was three," Asher said haughtily. "And I'm not the least affected."

Ty had no trouble recognizing the signs—the flushed cheeks, the glowing eyes and misty smile. Whatever she might say, he knew the champagne was swimming in her head. And when they loved again, she would be soft and strong and passionate. He found himself wanting to simply look at her for a few minutes more. Once they touched, the fire would take them.

"Want another?" he offered.

"Sure."

Wisely he filled her glass only halfway before he replaced the bottle. "I caught your interview today," Ty commented. "It was on while I was changing."

"Oh?" Asher shifted to lie on her stomach, propping herself on her elbows. "How'd I do?"

"Hard to say. It was all in French."

She laughed, adjusting her position so that she could take another sip. "I'd forgotten."

"How about a translation?"

"He asked things like—Mademoiselle Wolfe, do you find any changes in your style after your temporary retirement? And I said something like I feel I've tightened my serve." She chuckled into her wine. "I didn't mention that my muscles beg for me to give them a break after two sets. He asked how I felt about playing the *young* Miss Kingston in the finals and I refrained from punching him in the mouth."

"That was diplomatic," Ty answered, slipping the glass from her fingers.

"I'm a hell of a diplomat," Asher agreed. Rolling over on her back, she looked up at him. He lounged just behind her so that she had to tilt her head at an odd angle to make eye contact. "You stole my glass."

"Yes, I did." After setting it on the tray, Ty gave the wheeled table a slight shove.

"Did we finish dinner?" Reaching up and back, she locked her arms around his neck.

"We've definitely finished dinner." He allowed her to urge him down until his mouth hovered above hers.

"Got any suggestions about what we should do now?" She liked the strangeness of having his face upside down over hers. Playfully she nipped at his lip.

"No. Do you?"

"Got a deck of cards?"

"Uh-uh."

"Then I guess we'll have to make love." She gave a rich, low laugh before she kissed him again. "All night—just to pass the time."

"It's something to do. Rainy nights are so boring."

Eyes dancing, she nodded. "Mmm, yes. Let's make the best of it."

Her lips were curved in a smile as his met them, but they parted eagerly. She found it strangely seductive to have his tongue meet hers this way. On a gurgle of laughter, she closed her teeth gently, capturing him. In response, he trailed his fingers over her breast until her moan freed him.

"I get dizzy kissing you upside down," Asher murmured.

"I like you dizzy." Leaning forward, he trailed moist kisses over her throat. The tip of his tongue picked up her flavor, then lingered over it. He could feel pulse beats both with his hand and his lips. Finding the curve of his neck vulnerable, Asher began to give him the same pleasure he was bringing her.

"I want to touch you," she complained. "I can't touch you this way."

But he continued to explore from where he was, enjoying the freedom his hands had over her body. The scent of the rich sauce still lingered in the air, and the zing of champagne clung to two tongues as they joined. The mattress groaned quietly as she shifted. Then she was on her knees, pressed body to body. In a quick move she had stripped the robe from him so he was as naked as she. With a half laugh, half sigh, she ran her palms up his strong back.

Entwined, enchanted, neither noticed that the

rain had ceased. Inside the quiet room, pleasure built. Strong thigh pressed against strong thigh, hungry lips sought hungry lips. Their passion was equal, their needs the same. Together, they lay down.

Soft sighs became moans. Before long, gentle caresses became demanding. Both seemed desperate to touch and be touched, to have their own weaknesses exploited. With instinctive understanding they held back the final gift. The inner fire built, dampening their flesh, but still they lingered over each other. There was so much to make up for, so much time to recapture. Though passion was flaring, this thought hovered in the back of both their minds. Tonight was a fresh beginning. They wanted all of it.

Asher thought her lungs would burst. The combination of wine and passion buzzed in her head. A laugh, smoky with desire, floated from her as he gasped her name. She wanted to tempt him, torment him, give to him. His stomach was hard and flat with muscle, yet the touch of her fingertip could make it quiver. Asher had forgotten this sense of power and exulted in it. Her small hands could make him weak. Her shapely, serious mouth could drive him wild.

The power shifted so abruptly, she was helpless. He found her greatest vulnerability and used his tongue to destroy her last vestige of control. Half wild, she called for him, struggling to have more, desperate to have all. Arching, she pressed him closer, cresting on a wave of delight that had no chance to recede. She thrashed as if in protest, yet arched again in invitation. As she built toward a higher peak, Ty slid up her body. Greedy, she drew him inside of her, hearing his gasp for breath before there was only feeling.

Later, they still clung together, damp, spent, fulfilled. He shifted only to turn out the light. In the midnight darkness they molded to each other, drifting toward sleep.

"You'll move in with me."

The murmur was a statement rather than a question. Asher opened her eyes before she answered. She could just see the outline of his face. "Yes, if you want me."

"I never stopped wanting you."

Without the light he didn't see the flicker of doubt in her eyes before he slept.

Chapter Seven

She was afraid of London. Lady Wickerton had lived there—hostessing parties in the elegant three-story house in Grosvenor Square, attending the ballet at the Royal Opera House, the theater in Drury Lane, shopping in the West End. Lady Wickerton had played bridge with members of Parliament and had sipped tea at Buckingham Palace. Lady Wickerton had been a quiet, dutiful wife, a woman of intelligence, breeding and control. She had nearly suffocated in London.

Perhaps if Ty hadn't come between Jim Wolfe's daughter and Eric Wickerton's wife, Asher would have accepted her role with ease. She'd wanted to, had struggled to. Too much passion simmered inside her. It had been there all of her life, but the months with Ty had liberated it. Controlling something dormant was entirely different from harnessing something that pulsed with life. There had not even been her profession as an outlet for the energy that drove her.

Coming back to London was the most difficult step yet. There she would not only have to face memories of Ty, but the ghost of the woman she had pretended to be. It was all so familiar—Westminster Abbey, Trafalgar Square, the smells, the voices. Even the anticipation of Wimbledon couldn't block them out. There would be faces here that would remember the coolly elegant Lady Wickerton. And there would be questions.

Publicly she would remain aloof, distant and uninformative. Asher felt she owed Eric that much. She would simply refuse to discuss her marriage or its demise. Her early training, her years of following her father's rules, would serve her now more than ever.

She would give them tennis. With two straight championships now under her belt, Asher would have been spotlighted in any case. It was up to her to sway the press away from her personal life toward her professional resurgence. What was growing between her and Ty was still too fragile to be shared.

Happiness. She had nearly forgotten how simple and overwhelming the feeling was. Lazy midnight talks, crazy loving, quiet walks. They shared a hotel room and made it home for the days and nights they were there. She felt as much a Gypsy as he, and was content to be so. Once she had looked for roots, stability, commitment. She'd learned that they meant nothing without the fullness of love. His spontaneity had always fascinated her. This time Asher would resolve the lingering fear of it and enjoy.

"Aren't you dressed yet?"

At the question Asher stopped tying her tennis shoe and glanced up. Ty stood in the doorway between the small parlor and bedroom. Fully dressed, impatient, he frowned at her. His hair fell over his forehead as unruly as ever and still slightly damp from his shower. Waves of love radiated through her.

"Nearly," Asher tossed back. "Not everyone can move quickly in the morning, you know—especially on six hours sleep."

The frown became a grin. "Something keep you up?" He caught the shoe she hurled at him in one hand, his eyes never leaving her face. Apparently the late night hadn't affected him. He looked well rested and full of barely controlled energy. "You can always take a nap after morning practice."

"Awfully pleased with yourself this morning, aren't you?"

"Am I?" Still grinning, he came toward her, tossing her shoe lightly. "It probably has something to do with trouncing that British kid in the quarterfinals yesterday."

"Oh?" Lifting a brow, Asher looked up at him. "Is that all you're pleased about?"

"What else?"

"Let me have my shoe," she demanded. "So I can throw it at you again."

"Did you know you have a poor morning attitude?" he asked, holding the shoe out of reach.

"Did you know you've been insufferable ever since you won the French?" she countered sweetly. "Remember, it's only one quarter of the Grand Slam."

He moved the shoe farther out of reach as she made a grab for it. "For you too, Face," he reminded her.

"The rest's on grass." In an attempt to hold him still, Asher grabbed the waistband of his warm-up pants.

"The woman's insatiable," he sighed. Diving, he pinned her beneath him on the bed.

"Ty! Stop!" Laughing, Asher pushed against him as he nuzzled at her neck. "We'll be late for practice."

"Oh. You're right." Giving her a quick kiss, he rolled away from her.

"Well," Asher muttered as she sat up, "you didn't take much persuading." Even as she started to tidy her hair, she was spun back into his arms. Her startled exclamation was smothered by his lips.

Long, deep, infinitely tender, smolderingly passionate. His arms encircled her. Asher felt her bones soften, then dissolve. Her head fell back, inviting him to take more. Cradling her, Ty went on a slow exploration of her mouth. For the moment he enjoyed the sense of total domination. If they continued, he knew she would begin her own demands. Then it would be power for power. The knowledge excited him. Still, he laughed against her lips. There was time. A lifetime.

"You awake yet?" he asked her as he ran a hand lightly over her breast.

"Mmm-hmm."

"Good. Let's go." After setting her on her feet, he gave Asher's bottom a friendly pat.

"I'll get you for that," she promised. Needs stirred inside her, not quite under control.

"I certainly hope so." With an easy smile Ty slipped an arm around her shoulders. "You need to work on your backhand volley," he began as they walked from the room.

Insulted, Asher tossed her head back. "What are you talking about?"

"If you'd shorten your swing a bit more—"

"Shorten your own swing," she retorted. "And while you're at it," she continued, "you weren't exactly Mr. Speed yesterday."

"Gotta save something for the finals."

Asher snorted as she punched the elevator button. "Your conceit never wavers."

"Confidence," Ty contradicted. He liked seeing her this way—relaxed, but ready to laugh or to slap back. Briefly he wondered if she realized she was even more beautiful when she forgot caution. "What about breakfast?"

"What about it?"

"Want to grab some eggs after practice?"

She slid her eyes to his as the doors opened. "Is that your best offer?"

Ty lifted a brow as he followed her into the elevator. Asher exchanged a polite nod with a middle-aged couple in tweed. "Maybe you'd like to take up where we left off last night?" Ty lounged against an elevator wall as Asher gaped at him. "What did you say your name was again?"

Asher could feel two pairs of shocked and interested eyes boring into her back. "Misty," she replied, allowing a trace of cockney to color her voice. "Will you spring for champagne again, Mr. Starbuck? It was ever so good."

He recognized the light of challenge in her eyes and grinned. "So were you, sweetie."

When the doors opened to the lobby, the older couple moved out reluctantly. Asher punched Ty in the arm before she followed.

In less than an hour they were both concentrating on form and speed and the capricious bounces a ball could take on grass. Was she playing better? Asher wondered as she sprang for Madge's slice. She felt looser, less encumbered. Indeed, she felt as though losing were not even a possibility. At Wimbledon she could forget the city of London.

Instead, she could remember the qualifying games at Roehampton, with their anything-goes attitude. Both bad language and rackets had flown. It was a contrast to the elegance and glamour of Wimbledon. Here both the players and the crowd were steeped in tradition. Hydrangeas against a backdrop of rich green grass, ivy-covered walls, limos and chauffeurs. Colors were soothing, mauve and green, as if time itself had sobered them.

Here spectators would be well-mannered, quiet between points, applauding after them. Even those in standing room would behave, or the chair judge would tell them politely to quiet down. No one hung from the scoreboards at Wimbledon. It was as revered as the changing of the guards, as English as double-decker buses.

There was no doubt, as one gazed around the immaculately tended velvet lawns, the pampered roses, the dollhouse kiosks and the stands that could accommodate more than twenty-five thousand, that Wimbledon *was* tennis. It was here former players migrated to. It was here future players aspired to. Asher remembered Ty telling her about watching the matches one long-ago July Fourth and making a vow. He had kept it, not once, but four times. More than anything she had wanted before, Asher wanted them to both walk away from Centre Court as champions.

Behind the baseline, Asher stood with a racket and a ball, staring off into space.

"Had enough?" Madge called out.

"Hmm . . . what?" Asher's head snapped around. Seeing Madge standing with her legs spread, hand on hips, had her laughing. "I suppose I have, I was daydreaming."

From opposite ends of the court, they walked toward their bags and jackets. "No sense asking if you're happy," Madge began conversationally. "You look absolutely miserable floating two inches off the ground."

"That obvious, huh?"

"I won't pretend not to be pleased," Madge added smugly. "I've always thought you two made a great team. Going to make it official?"

"I—No, we're just taking it one day at a time." Asher kept her eyes lowered as she packed her racket. "Marriage is just a formality, after all."

"And pigs fly," Madge countered calmly. When Asher glanced up with a cautious smile, she went on. "For some, yes, you're right. Not for you, Face. Why did you stay in an unhappy marriage for three years?" When Asher started to speak, Madge lifted a hand. "Because to you marriage is a promise, and you don't break promises."

"I failed once," she began.

"Oh, all by yourself? Isn't that being a bit self-absorbed?" Impatient, Madge settled her hands on her hips again. "Listen, you aren't going to let one mistake keep you from being happy, are you?"

"I am happy," Asher assured her, punctuating the statement by touching Madge's shoulder. "Ty's all I've ever wanted, Madge, I can't risk losing him again."

Her brow puckered in confusion. "But you left him, Asher, not the other way around."

"I'd already lost him," she said flatly.

"Asher, I don't—"

"It's a new day," she interrupted, then took a deep breath of scented morning air. "A fresh start. I know what mistakes I made and have no intention of repeating them. There was a time in my life that I thought I had to come first, before this." Holding up the small white ball, Asher examined it. "Before anything. I looked on tennis as a competitor, his family as a rival. That was stupid." Dropping the ball into a can, Asher closed it.

"That's funny," Madge mused. "There was a time in my life I thought The Dean's work came first. He thought the same about me. It wasn't true in either case."

With a smile Asher slung her bag over her shoulder. "Ty won't ever forget that tennis took him out of that tenement. Maybe he shouldn't. That's the thing that brings fire to his game."

She knows him so well in some ways, Madge thought, and not at all in others. "And what brings the ice to yours?"

"Fear," Asher answered before she thought. For a moment she gave Madge a blank look, then shrugged. Saying it aloud made it seem rather unimportant. "Fear of failure, or exposure." Laughing, she began to walk. "Thank God you're not a reporter."

The gravel crunched underfoot as they moved down the path. It was a sound Asher associated with the tidiness of English courts. "Remind me to tell you sometime what goes through my head five minutes before a match."

With a sigh Asher hooked her arm through her old partner's. "Let's hit the showers."

There was no dream. Asher slept as deeply as a child, with no worries, no nagging fears. The curtains were drawn closed so that the afternoon sun filtered through lazily. Traffic sounds muffled through it, coming as a quiet drone. She wore only a short terry robe and lay on top of the spread. Ty would come back to wake her so that they could spend some time sight-seeing before nightfall. Because they were both scheduled to play the following day, they would go to bed early.

The knock on the door wakened her. Sitting up,

Asher ran a hand through her tousled hair. He'd forgotten his key, she thought groggily. She stepped from the dim bedroom into the brighter parlor, wincing against the change of light. Absently she wondered what time it was as she opened the door. Shock took a moment to penetrate.

"Eric," she whispered.

"Asher." He gave her what was nearly a bow before he elbowed his way into the room. "Did I wake you?"

"I was napping." She closed the door, trying to recover her scattered wits. He looked the same, she thought. Naturally he would. Eric would see no reason to change. He was tall, slim, with a military carriage. He had a sharp-featured European face, a bit haughty and remote. Dark blond hair was cut and groomed to indicate wealth and conservatism. Light eyes in a pale face—both romantic, intelligent and cold. Asher knew that his mouth could twist into a hard line when he was crossed. As a suitor he had been charming, as a lover, meticulous. As a husband he'd been unbearable. She drew herself straight. He was no longer her husband.

"I didn't expect to see you, Eric."

"No?" He smiled. "Did you think I wouldn't drop by while you were in town? Lost a bit of weight, Asher."

"Competition tends to do that." Years of training had her gesturing toward a chair. "Please, sit down. I'll get you a drink."

There was no reason to be upset by him now, she told herself. No need to feel fear or guilt. Divorced couples managed to be civilized more often than not. Eric, Asher thought with a grim smile, was a very civilized man.

"Have you been well?" She poured his scotch neat, then added ice to Perrier for herself.

"Quite well. And you?"

"Yes. Your family?"

"Doing wonderfully." Eric accepted the glass she offered, then eyed her over the rim. "And your father?" He watched for the flash of pain, and was satisfied.

"As far as I know, he's fine." Quite consciously Asher drew on the mask as she sat.

"Still hasn't forgiven you for giving up your career."

Her eyes were level now and expressionless. "I'm sure you're aware he hasn't."

Mindful of the crease in his pants, Eric crossed his legs. "I thought perhaps now that you're competing again . . ." He allowed the sentence to die.

Asher watched the bubbles rise in her glass, but left them untasted. "He no longer acknowledges me," she said flatly. "I'm still paying, Eric." She lifted her eyes again. "Does that satisfy you?"

He drank leisurely for a moment. "It was your choice, my dear. Your career for my name."

"For your silence," Asher corrected. "I already had your name."

"And another man's child in your belly."

Ice clinked against ice as her hands shook. Quickly she controlled the tremor. "One would have thought it would have been enough that I lost the child," she murmured. "Did you come all this way to remind me?"

"I came," Eric said as he leaned back, "to see how my ex-wife was adjusting. You're victorious on the courts, Asher, and as lovely as ever." She didn't speak as his eyes roamed the room. "Apparently you didn't waste too much time picking up with your old lover."

"My mistake was in leaving him, Eric. We both know that. I'm very, very sorry."

He sent her an icy look. "Your mistake was in trying to pass his bastard off on me."

Furious and trembling, Asher sprang to her feet. "I never lied to you. And by God, I'll never apologize again."

He remained seated, swirling liquor. "Does he know yet?"

Her color drained dramatically enough to make him smile genuinely. Hate ate at him. "No, I see he doesn't. How interesting."

"I kept my word, Eric." Though her hands were laced tightly together, Asher's voice was strong. "As long as I was your wife, I did everything you asked of me."

He acknowledged this with a slight nod. Her honesty hadn't been enough—nor had her three years of penance. "But you're not my wife any longer."

"We agreed. The marriage was intolerable for both of us."

"What are you afraid he'd do?" Eric mused, frowning up at the ceiling. "He's a very physical man

as I remember, with a primitive sort of temper."
Lowering his eyes, he smiled again. "Do you think
he'd beat you?"

Asher gave a short laugh. "No."

"You're very confident," he murmured. "What
exactly are you afraid of?"

Wearily she dropped her hands to her sides. "He
wouldn't forgive me, Eric, any more than you have.
I lost the child, I lost my father. My self-esteem. I'll
never lose the guilt. I hurt nothing but your pride,
Eric, haven't I suffered enough for that?"

"Perhaps . . . perhaps not." Rising, he stepped
toward her. She remembered the scent of his crisp,
dignified cologne very well. "Perhaps the most perfect punishment might be in never knowing your
secret is safe. I'll make you no promises, Asher."

"It astonishes me that I was ever naïve enough to
think you a kind man, Eric," she said softly.

"Justice," he returned, toasting her.

"Revenge has little to do with justice."

He shrugged an elegant shoulder. "All in your
viewpoint, my dear."

She wouldn't give him the satisfaction of breaking
down—of weeping, of screaming or begging. Instead, Asher stood perfectly still. "If you've said all
you've come to say, I'd like you to go."

"Of course." After finishing off the liquor, he set
down the glass. "Sleep well, darling. Don't bother,
I'll let myself out." Eric turned the doorknob and
found himself face to face with Ty. Nothing could
have pleased him more.

Ty noted his cold, satisfied smile before his gaze

shifted to Asher. Standing in the center of the room, she seemed frozen. There was anguish, and, he thought, fear in her eyes. Her face was dead-white and still. Even as he wondered what it was she feared, Ty took in the rest of her appearance. The tousled hair, the brief robe and exposed skin had rage boiling in him. Asher could feel it from where she stood.

His eyes whipped back to Eric's. There was murder in them. "Get the hell out of here."

"Just on my way," Eric said equably, though he had inched back against the door in instinctive defense. His last thought as he shut it behind him was that Asher would bear the brunt of the fury in Ty's eyes. That alone had made it worth the trip.

The room vibrated with the silent storm. Asher didn't move. It seemed Ty would stare at her for eternity. The trembling was difficult to control, but she forced herself. If she made light of the incident, perhaps so would he.

"What the hell was he doing here?"

"He just dropped by . . . I suppose to wish me luck." The lie sliced at her.

"Cozy." Crossing to her, Ty caught the lapel of her robe in his hand. "Don't you usually dress for visitors, Asher? Then again, I suppose it isn't necessary for ex-husbands."

"Ty, don't."

"Don't what?" he demanded. Though he struggled against the words, the accusations, the feelings, he knew it was a losing battle. Against the unknown he would always attack. "Wouldn't it be better form to meet him somewhere else? It's a little sticky here, isn't it?"

The cold sarcasm hurt more than his fury would have. With so much to hide, she could only shake her head. "Ty, you know there's nothing between us. You know—"

"What the hell do I know?" he shouted, grasping the other lapel. "Don't ask, don't question. Then I walk in and find you entertaining the bastard you left me for."

"I didn't know he was coming." She gripped his arms for balance as he nearly lifted her off her feet. "If he had called, I would have told him to stay away."

"You let him in." Enraged, he shook her. "Why?"

Despair rather than fear clutched at her. "Would you be happier if I had slammed the door in his face?"

"Yes, damn it."

"I didn't." She pushed at him now, as furious as he. "I let him in, I gave him a drink. Make what you like of it. I can't stop you."

"Did he want you back?" he demanded, ignoring her struggles. "Is that why he came?"

"What does it matter?" Impotently she slammed her fists into his chest. "It's not what *I* want." She threw back her head, her eyes burning.

"Then tell me, tell me now why you married him." When she tried to pull away, he dragged her back. "I'll have that much, Asher, and I'll have it now."

"Because I thought he was what I needed," she

cried out. Roaring in her ears was the anger, the fear she had felt for Eric.

"And was he?" To prevent her from striking out, Ty grasped her wrist.

"No!" She jerked but couldn't free herself. Frustration added to an almost unreasonable fury. "No, I was miserable. I was trapped." Her voice was both strong and harsh. "I paid in ways you can't imagine. There wasn't a day I was happy. Does that satisfy you?"

She did something he had never seen her do before. She wept. His grip on her wrists loosened as he watched tears flood her eyes and spill onto her cheeks. Never in all the years he'd known her had he seen that kind of torment on her face. Tearing herself from his grip, Asher fled into the bedroom, slamming the door at her back.

She wanted peace. She wanted privacy. The grief had hit her unexpectedly. If the tears hadn't clogged her throat, she would have told him about the baby. The words had been there, ready to spill out in anger. Then speech had been impossible. Now she needed to weep it out.

Ty stared at the closed door for a long time. The wrenching sound of sobbing came to him. It was a reaction he hadn't expected. His anger was justified, as were his questions. Anger for anger he could have comprehended, but the pain he heard was altogether different. Having come from a family of women, he understood woman's tears. Over the years he'd done his share of comforting and soothing. But these sobs were hot and bitter—and Asher never wept.

Jess cried easily, quiet, feminine tears. His mother wept with joy or silent sadness. These he could handle. A shoulder could be offered, a few sympathetic words, a teasing comment. Instinctively he knew none of those were the prescription for raw grief.

He still had questions. He still had anger. But the sounds from the bedroom forced him to put them aside. Ty recognized when tears were used as a weapon or a defense. These were being torn from her unwillingly. Dragging a hand through his hair, he wondered if it was Eric or himself who was responsible for them. Or something he knew nothing about. Cursing softly, he went to the door and opened it.

She lay curled on the bed in a ball of misery. Her body shook. When he touched her she jerked away. Saying nothing, Ty lay down beside her, gathering her close. For another moment she fought him. *Alone.* Her tears were not to be observed, not to be shared. *Private.* Ty dealt with her struggles by merely holding her tighter in arms that were both strong and gentle.

"I'm not going anywhere," he murmured.

With no more protest, Asher clung to his comfort and let her grief run its course.

It had grown dark and her body was weak. There were no more tears left in her. Ty's arms were strong around her. Beneath her damp cheek she could hear the steady beat of his heart. Gently, almost absently, his fingers stroked the base of her neck.

She'd nearly told him. Asher closed her eyes, too

weary to feel fear or regret. If she could have summoned up the energy, she would have been grateful for the tears that had prevented her confession.

I lost your baby. Would he be holding her now if those words had spilled out? What good would it do to tell him? she asked herself. Why make him grieve for something he had never known? And grieve he would, she knew, after the anger passed. It came to her suddenly that it wasn't only fear that kept the secret locked inside her. She couldn't bear to see Ty hurt as she had hurt.

How could she explain to him about Eric without dragging up old bitterness, opening old wounds? Ty hadn't wanted her any longer—Jess had made that abundantly clear. But Eric had. It had been her pride that had turned to Eric, then her sense of duty that had kept her with him. Perhaps if she had been stronger after the accident she would never have made those promises to him. . . .

Asher had floated to consciousness on a wave of pain. What reason was there to wake up and hurt? she thought groggily. Sleep, sleep was so peaceful.

She remembered the shouting, the fall, the swimming darkness. The baby . . . Ty's baby. Panic—the panic pierced her lethargy. Her eyelids seemed weighted with lead, but she forced them open even as she reached a protective hand to her stomach. Stern and cold, Eric's face floated in front of her eyes.

"The baby," she managed through dry lips.

"Dead."

Tearing, burning grief replaced the pain. "No." Moaning, she closed her eyes again. "Oh, God, no. My baby, not my baby. Ty—"

"Listen to me, Asher." Eric spoke briskly. For three days he had waited while Asher drifted in and out of consciousness. She had lost the baby and a great deal of blood. Once she had nearly slipped away, but he had willed her to live. The love he had once felt had turned to resentment that bordered on hate. She had deceived him, made a fool of him. Now he would have his payment.

"My baby . . ."

"The baby's dead," he said flatly, then gripped her hand. "Look at me." She obeyed with eyes glazed with sorrow. "You're in a private clinic. The reason for your being here will never be known beyond the front doors. If you do what I say."

"Eric . . ." A spark of hope flickered. With what strength she had, Asher tightened her fingers on his. "Are they sure? Couldn't there be a mistake? Please—"

"You miscarried. The servants will be discreet. As far as anyone knows, we've slipped away for a few days."

"I don't understand." She pressed her hand against her stomach as if to make the truth a lie. "The fall . . . I fell down the stairs. But—"

"An accident," he stated, making the loss of the child sound like a broken glass.

Insidiously the pain slipped through. "Ty," Asher moaned, shutting her eyes.

"You're my wife, and will remain so until I say differently." Eric waited until her eyes focused on him again. "Would you have me call your lover and tell him you married me while carrying his child?"

"No." She could only whisper the word. *Ty.* She ached for him. He was lost to her—as lost as the child they'd made together.

"Then you'll do as I say. You'll retire from professional tennis. I won't have the press speculating about the two of you and dragging my name through the mud. You'll behave as I expect Lady Wickerton to behave. I will not touch you," he continued with a trace of disgust. "Any physical desire I felt for you is gone. We will live in the manner I designate or your lover will hear from me about this game you played. Is this understood?"

What did it matter how she lived? Asher asked herself. She was already dead. "Yes. I'll do whatever you want. Please, leave me alone now."

"As you wish." He rose. "When you're stronger, you'll give an official press release on your retirement. Your reason will be that you have no more time for tennis or any desire for a career that would take you away from your husband and your adopted country."

"Do you think it matters to me?" she whispered. "Just let me alone, let me sleep."

"Your word, Asher."

She gave him a long last look before she wearily closed her eyes. "My word, Eric."

And she had kept it. She had tolerated Eric's pleasure when her father had turned away from her. She had ignored his discreet but frequent affairs. For months she had lived like a zombie, doing as she was bid. When the layers of grief began to peel away, his hold remained through guilt and threats. When she had begun to come to life again, Asher had bargained for her freedom. Nothing was more important to Eric than his reputation. She held his many women in one hand, he held the knowledge of Ty's child in the other. They'd made an uneasy agreement.

Now he was back, Asher mused. Perhaps because she was making a success of her life again. Still, she felt he would keep his silence, if only to ensure a hold over her. Once he spoke, all ties were severed. Or if she spoke . . .

She remembered the look on Ty's face when he had seen her with Eric. Explanations would never be accepted now. Perhaps the day would come when they fully trusted each other, when the memory of betrayal would be dimmed.

She'd been silent for some time. By the steadiness of her breathing she might have been sleeping. Ty knew she was awake and thinking. What secrets was she holding from him? he wondered. And how long would it be before the air between them was finally cleared? He wanted to demand, but her vulnerability prevented him. More than anything else, he didn't want to risk her slipping behind the wall she could so easily erect.

"Better?" he murmured.

She sighed before he felt the faint movement of her head as she nodded. There was one thing she could settle between them, one thing she could make him understand. "Ty, he means nothing to me. Do you believe that?"

"I want to."

"Believe it." Suddenly intense, she sat up and leaned against his chest. If she could give him nothing else, she could give him this. "I feel nothing for Eric, not even hate. The marriage was a mistake. From the start it was nothing more than a façade."

"Then why—"

"It's always been you," she said before she crushed her mouth to his. "Always you." She pressed her lips to his throat, passion erupting in her as swiftly as the tears. "I stopped living for so long and now . . ." Her mouth ran wildly over his face. "I need you now, only you."

Her mouth met his fervently, saying more than words. Her ardor touched off his own. There was no need for questions now, or for answers. She pulled the shirt from him, eager to touch. Pressing her lips to heated flesh, she heard him groan. Though her hands moved swiftly to undress him, her lips loitered, lingering to arouse. With her tongue she left a moist trail of fire.

His body was a pleasure to her—hard muscle, long bones, taut flesh. Delighting in him, she sought new secrets. If she nibbled at his waist, his breathing grew shallow, his fingers gripped her hair. If she moved her palm along his thigh, his moan vibrated with need. Giddy with power, she ran a crazed trail from stomach to chest, her lips hungry and seeking.

He struggled to pull the robe from her as she caught his earlobe between her teeth. Low, sultry laughter drove him wild. Neither heard the seam rip as he tugged the terry cloth from her. Limber and quick, she made it impossible for him to grant them both the final relief. Her lovemaking tormented and thrilled him while her agility held him off.

"Now," he demanded, grasping her hips. "Asher, for God's sake."

"No, no, no," she murmured, then cut off his oath with a searing kiss. She found the torture exquisite. Though her own body begged for fulfillment, she wanted to prolong it. As his hands slid over her damp skin, she arched back, reveling in his touch. She belonged, and always would, to the man who could release her fires.

Neither was in control, each a slave to the other. She wanted nothing more than to be bound to him—here, in a dark room with the sound of her own breathing raging in her ears, in the sunlight with the secrets of the night still humming between them. For always.

Beneath her, his body was hot and moist and moving. The rhythm seduced her. Everything warm, everything giving, flowed through her. Thoughts vanished, memories dimmed. Now—there was only now—the all-powerful, greedy present.

This time when he gripped her hips she made no attempt to stop him. Her head fell back in complete abandonment as they joined. The moan was rich and deep, and from both of them. As one, they were catapulted up, beyond pleasure, into ecstasy.

Chapter Eight

Asher had driven in limousines all her life. As a child she'd ridden behind a chauffeur named George in a shiny maroon car with smoked glass and a built-in bar. George had remained the family driver though the cars had changed—an elegant white Rolls, a sturdy blue Mercedes.

Lady Wickerton's driver had been Peter and the car had been an old discreet gray Daimler. Peter had been as silent and as efficient as the car. Asher felt no thrill at being driven in the long black limo toward Wimbledon.

As they passed through Roehampton, she watched the scenery. Tidy, healthy trees, trimmed shrubs, orderly flowers. In a few hours, she would be on Centre Court. Aching, sweating . . . and winning. This was the big prize. Credibility, prestige, press. They were all at Wimbledon.

Once before she and Ty had taken the championships and led the dancing at the Wimbledon Ball—in that year of her life that had brought complete joy and complete misery. Now she would play her old foe Maria Rayski with all the verve and all the cunning she had at her disposal.

Though she'd thought her life had begun to come to order with her first win, Asher now realized she'd been wrong. The turning point was today, here in the arena that was synonymous with her profession. She would play her best here, on the surface she knew best, in the country in which she had lived like a prisoner. Perhaps true confidence would begin after this match was over.

She thought of Ty, the young boy who had once vowed to play and win. Now, in the lush interior of the limo, Asher made a similar vow. She would have a championship season. Reestablish Asher Wolfe *for* Asher Wolfe. Then she would be ready to face the woman. The woman would face the only man who mattered.

The crowds waited for her and other arriving players. The greetings were enthusiastic. Roaming spectators sipped champagne or nibbled on strawberries and cream. Signing autographs, Asher felt light, confident, ready. Nothing, she thought, could mar such a day. The Fourth of July, the brilliant sunshine, the scent of garden flowers.

She remembered other Wimbledons. So little had changed. Fans mingled with players, chatting, laughing. The atmosphere was one of an informal tea party with the promise of a spectacle. But she could feel the nerves. They were there, just under the bonhomie, in the young players, the veterans, doubles and singles finalists. Mixing among them were rock stars and celebrities, millionaires and landed gentry.

Asher saw faces from the past, players from her father's generation. For them it was a reunion, nostalgia, tradition. There were people she had entertained in Grosvenor Square. For them it was a social event. The dress was summer-garden-party chic—picture hats and pastels. Because yesterdays had to be faced, Asher greeted former acquaintances.

"Asher, how lovely to see you again. . . ." "What a sweet little outfit. . . ." "How strange it is not to see you at the club anymore. . . ." There was speculation thinly veiled by manners. She dealt with it calmly, as she had during her three years of marriage.

"Where's that old man of yours?"

Turning, Asher clasped two large hands warmly. "Stretch McBride, you haven't changed a bit."

Of course he had. When he'd first tickled Asher's chin, he'd been thirty. His face had been unlined, his hair untouched with gray. He'd won nearly every major championship there was to win twice around. Though he was still tall, and nearly as lean as he had been in his prime, the twenty years showed on his face.

"You always told a lie beautifully." Grinning, he kissed her cheek. "Where's Jim?"

"In the States," she answered, keeping her smile bright. "How have you been, Stretch?"

"Just fine. Got five grandchildren and a nice string

of sporting goods stores on the East Coast." He patted her hand. "Don't tell me Jim isn't going to be here? He hasn't missed it in forty years."

It was a struggle not to show the pain, much less not to feel it. "As far as I know, he won't be. I'm awfully glad to see you again. I haven't forgotten that you taught me the dump shot."

Pleased, he laughed. "Use it on Maria today," he advised. "I love to see Americans win at Wimbledon. Tell your old man hello for me."

"Take care, Stretch." Her smile evaded the promise she couldn't give. With a parting kiss, he moved away.

Turning, Asher found herself face to face with Lady Daphne Evans. The striking brunette had been one of Eric's less discreet dalliances, and one of Asher's more difficult trials. Her eyes automatically cooled, though her voice was scrupulously polite.

"Daphne, you look exquisite."

"Asher." Daphne skimmed cool eyes over Asher's brief tennis dress, down long bare legs to her court shoes. "You look different. How odd to find you an athlete."

"Odd?" Asher countered. "I've always been an athlete. Tell me, how is your husband?"

The thrust was parried with a quick laugh. "Miles is in Spain on business. As it happens, Eric escorted me today."

Though her stomach churned, her face remained composed. "Eric's here?"

"Yes, of course." Meticulously Daphne adjusted the brim of her rose-pink hat. "You don't think he'd miss this Wimbledon, do you?" Long mink lashes swept down, then up again. "We're all very interested in the results. Will we see you at the ball, darling?"

"Naturally."

"Well, I must let you mingle, mustn't I? That's traditional. Best of luck." With a flash of a smile Daphne swirled her skirts and was gone.

Asher fought the nausea, but began to nudge her way through the crowd. All she wanted was the comparative peace of the A locker rooms. The day ahead promised to be enough of a fight without contending with ghosts. With a few smiles and mechanically gracious greetings, she made her way out of the main throng. A few moments to herself—that was what she needed before the stands began to fill, before her strength and abilities were put to the test.

She knew Eric well enough to be certain he had asked Daphne to seek her out. Yes, he would want to be sure she knew he was there—before the match. As she slipped into the locker room, Asher noticed her hands were shaking. She couldn't allow it. In thirty minutes she would have to be in complete control.

When she walked onto the court Asher was careful not to look into the crowd. It would be easier on her nerves if the people who watched and cheered remained anonymous. As she attempted to empty her mind of all but the first game, Asher watched Maria Rayski.

On her own side of the court, Rayski paced, gesturing occasionally to the crowd, tossing comments. Her nerves were undisguised. It was always so, Asher mused. Rayski chewed her nails, cracked her knuckles and said the first thing that came into her mind. In a wary sort of fashion Asher had always liked her. At five foot ten, she was tall for a woman and rangy, with a deadly stretch. Fatalistically Asher recalled she had a habit of badgering her opponent.

Well, she decided as she chose her game racket, Rayski's histronics might just keep her mind off who was, and who was not in the stands. She eyed the television camera dispassionately. With the wonder of technology, the match would be relayed to the States with only a brief delay. Would her father even bother to watch? she wondered. Silently she walked to the baseline for the first serve.

There was no cautious testing in the first games. Rayski went straight for the jugular. Both were fast players, and while Rayski was more aggressive, Asher was a better strategist. A ball could take ungodly bounces on grass, particularly the lush grass of Wimbledon's Centre Court. To defend, to attack, required instinct and timing. It also required complete concentration.

The lead jockeyed back and forth during the first set as the players gave the fourteen thousand spectators the show they'd come to see. Over the elegant, century-old court, they sweated, gritted their teeth and scrambled, not for the enjoyment of those who paid to see, but for the game. Rayski tossed an occasional taunt over the net between rallies. Asher might have been deaf for all the response she gave. She had her rhythm—nothing was going to interfere with it.

She placed her ground strokes with deadly precision, charged the net for short angling volleys. Both her form and her energy seemed at perfect peak.

Everything changed when the women took their seats for the towel-off before the third set.

Because she had forgotten about everything but the game, Asher's defenses were lowered. An inadvertent glance up in the stands had her eyes locking with Eric's. A slow, icy smile spread over his face as he lifted a hand in salute—or reminder.

What the devil's wrong with her? Ty asked himself. He shifted closer to the edge of his seat and studied Asher with narrowed eyes. She'd just dropped two games straight, the second one on a double fault. True, Rayski was playing superbly, but so had Asher—until the third set. She was playing mechanically now, as if the life had gone out of her. Too often she was missing basic shots or failing to put anything extra on a return. Rayski's serve was not her strongest weapon, yet she was repeatedly breezing service winners past Asher.

If he didn't know her better, he would have sworn Asher was tanking the match. But Asher wasn't capable of deliberately losing.

Carefully Ty watched for signs of an injury. A strained muscle or twisted ankle would explain the change in her. She gave no sign of favoring a leg. The composure on her face was as perfect as a mask. Too perfect, Ty reflected as the third game went to fifteen–love. Something was definitely wrong, but it wasn't physical. Disturbed, he quickly scanned the crowd.

There were dozens of faces he knew, some by name, some by reputation. There was an award-winning actor he'd once played a celebrity tourney with. Ty had found him an earthy man with a credible forehand. He recognized the ballet star because Asher had once dragged him to see *The Firebird*. Beside the ballerina was a country-western singer with a crossover hit. Ty passed over them, looking for an answer. He found it sitting near the Royal Box.

There was a cool, satisfied smile on Eric's face as he watched his ex-wife. Beside him, a thin, flashy woman in a rose-colored hat looked bored. Rage rose in Ty instantly. His first instinct was to yank Eric up by his five-hundred-dollar lapels and rearrange the expression on his face with his fists.

"Son of a bitch," he muttered, already rising. The hand that grasped his wrist was strong.

"Where are you going?" Madge demanded.

"To do something I should've done three years ago."

Still clinging to his arm, Madge twisted her head to follow the direction of his eyes. "Oh, boy," she said under her breath. Through her fingertips she could feel Ty's temper. Only briefly did she consider the personal satisfaction she would gain from letting Ty do what he wanted. "Hold on," she snapped between her teeth. "Listen to me. Punching him out isn't going to do anything for Asher."

"The hell it won't," he retorted. "You know why he's here."

"To upset her," Madge managed calmly enough.

"Obviously he's succeeding. Go talk to her." A strong man might have cringed from the blazing look Ty turned on her. Madge merely arched a brow. "You want to start a fight, Starbuck, do it after the match. I'll referee. Right now, use your head."

His control didn't come easily. Madge watched him struggle for it, lose it, then finally win. Though his eyes were still stormy, the hand under hers relaxed. "If talking doesn't work," he said flatly, "I'm going to break him in half."

"I'll hold your coat," she promised before Ty slipped away.

Knowing he'd have only a moment, Ty decided to use words sparingly—and make them count. After losing the game without making a point, Asher slumped into her chair. She didn't see Ty waiting for her.

"What the hell's wrong with you?"

Her head jerked up at the harsh tone. "Nothing." She was tired, already defeated as she mopped at the sweat on her face.

"You're handing the match to Rayski on a platter."

"Leave me alone, Ty."

"Going to give him the satisfaction of watching you fall apart in front of fourteen thousand people, Face?" There was sarcasm without a trace of sympathy in his voice. He noted the quick, almost indiscernible flash in her eyes. He'd wanted to see it. Always, she played better if there was anger beneath the ice.

"I never thought I'd see you tank a match."

"Go to hell." Whirling, she stalked back to the baseline. Nobody, she thought as she waited for Rayski to take position, nobody accused Asher Wolfe of tanking. Rayski crouched in her pendulum receiving stance while Asher gave the ball a few testing bounces. Tossing it, she drew back her racket and lunged. The effort of the serve came out in a force of breath. The finely pulverized chalk at the baseline rose on contact. Without giving the ace a thought, Asher took her stance for the next serve.

Her anger had teeth. She could feel it gnawing at her. A photographer zoomed in on her face and captured the contradictory placid expression and frosted eyes. Temper was energy. Asher flew across the court, striking the ball as if it were the enemy. Yet her battle was sternly controlled. No one watching her would realize that she cursed Ty with each stroke. No one but Ty himself. Satisfied, he watched her turn her fury on her opponent.

Oh, she was fabulous to see, he thought. Those long, slim legs, the strong shoulders. Her form was so smooth, so precise, yet beneath was that excitement, that smoldering passion. She was as she played, he mused, and wanted her. No one but he knew just how reckless she could be, just how abandoned. The thought had desire moving through him. She was the woman all men fantasized about—part lady, part wanton. And his, Ty told himself fiercely. Only his.

After watching Asher fire a backhand volley past Rayski, he glanced up. Eric's smile was gone. As if sensing the scrutiny, the Englishman looked down. The two men studied each other as the crowd

applauded Asher's game. Ty laughed, softly, insolently, then walked away.

Though the match held close to the last point, the
impetus Ty had instilled in her carried Asher to the
win. She was polite, even charming as she accepted
the Wimbledon plate. Inside she was raging. The joy
of victory couldn't penetrate the fury and resentment she was feeling. Ty had turned the tide of her
emotions away from Eric and onto himself.

She wanted to shout. She smiled and raised her
trophy for the crowd to see. She wanted to scream.
Politely she allowed the army of cameras to snap
her. Fatigue didn't touch her. The ache in her arm
might not have existed.

At last freeing herself from the press and well-
wishers, she simmered under the shower and
changed. Determination made her remain at Wimbledon to watch Ty's match. Stubbornness made her
refuse to admire his game. Eric was forgotten.
Asher's only thought was to vent her fury at the first
possible moment. It took five hard sets and two and
a half hours before Ty could claim his own trophy.

Asher left the stadium before the cheers had died.

He knew she'd be waiting for him. Even before Ty
slipped the key in the lock, he knew what to expect.
He looked forward to it. His adrenaline was still
flowing. Neither the shower nor the massage had
taken it from him. Wimbledon always affected him
this way. As long as he played, winning there would
be his first goal.

Now, the demanding games behind him, the win
still sweet, he felt like a knight returning home

victorious from the wars. His woman waited. But she wouldn't throw herself into his arms. She was going to scratch at him. Oh, yes, he was looking forward to it.

Grinning, Ty turned the knob. He had no more than shut the door behind him than Asher stormed out of the bedroom.

"Congratulations, Face," he said amiably. "Looks like I get first dance at the ball."

"How dare you say those things to me in the middle of a match?" she demanded. Eyes glittering, she advanced on him. "How dare you accuse me of tanking?"

Ty set his bag and rackets on a chair. "What do you call what you were doing?"

"Losing."

"Quitting," he corrected her. "You might as well have put up a sign."

"I've never quit!"

He lifted a brow. "Only for three years."

"Don't you dare throw that in my face." Raising both hands, she shoved him. Instead of being offended, he laughed. It pleased him enormously that he could rattle her control.

"You did good," he reminded her. "I couldn't take a chance on your losing." He gave her cheek an affectionate pinch. "I didn't want to open the ball with Maria."

"You conceited, overconfident louse!" She shoved him again. "Gramaldi almost took you. I wish he had." She shouted the lie at him. "You could use a good kick in the ego." With the intention of storming back into the bedroom, she whirled. Catching her wrist, Ty spun her back around.

"Aren't you going to congratulate me?"

"No."

"Aw, come on, Face." He grinned appealingly. "Give us a kiss."

For an answer Asher balled her hand into a fist. Ducking the blow, Ty gripped her waist and slung her over his shoulder. "I love it when you're violent," he said huskily as she pulled his hair.

To her own surprise—and annoyance—she had to choke back a laugh. "Then you're going to get a real charge out of this," she promised, kicking wildly as he threw her on the bed. Even though her reflexes were quick, Ty had her pinned beneath him in seconds. Breathless, she struggled to bring her knee up to his weakest point.

"Not that violent." Wisely he shifted to safety.

She twisted, squirmed and struggled. "You take your hands off me."

"Soon as I'm finished," he agreed, slipping a hand under the blouse that had come loose from her waistband.

Refusing to acknowledge the sensation of pleasure, Asher glared at him. "Don't you touch me."

"I have to touch you to make love to you." His smile was reasonable and friendly. "It's the only way I know how."

I will not laugh, she ordered herself as the gurgle rose in her throat. She was angry, furious, she reminded herself.

Ty recognized the weakening and capitalized on it.

"Your eyes get purple when you're mad. I like it."
He kissed her firmly shut mouth. "Why don't you
yell at me some more?"

"I have nothing more to say to you," Asher
claimed haughtily. "Please go away."

"But we haven't made love yet." Lightly he
rubbed his nose against hers.

Refusing to be charmed, she turned her head
away. "We aren't going to."

"Wanna bet?" With one swift move he ripped her
blouse from neck to waist.

"Ty!" Shocked, Asher gaped at him, her mouth
open.

"I nearly did that when you were on Centre Court
today. You should be glad I waited." Before she
could react he tore her shorts into two ragged pieces.
Thinking he might have gone mad, Asher stayed
perfectly still. "Something wrong?" he asked as his
hand moved to cup her breast.

"Ty, you can't tear my clothes."

"I already did." Soft as a feather, his hand roamed
down to her stomach. "Want to tear mine?"

"No." Her skin was beginning to quiver. She tried
to shift away and found herself held prisoner.

"I made you angry."

Her head cleared long enough for her to glare at
him. "Yes, and—"

"Angry enough to win," he murmured, trailing
his lips along her throat. "And when I watched you I
nearly exploded from wanting you. All that passion
simmering just under the surface. And I know what
it's like when it escapes."

She gave a little moan as his fingers stroked the point of her breast but tried to cling to reality. "You had no business saying I was tanking."

"I didn't say that, I only planted the idea." When he lifted his head, the look in his eyes had her drawing in a quick breath. "Did you think I'd stand by and watch him get to you like that? No man gets to you, Asher, no man but me."

With a savage kiss he cut off all words, all thoughts.

It always surprised Asher that Ty could project such raw sexuality in black tie. Conservative, formal dress could do nothing to alter his air of primitive masculinity. The material could cover the muscles, but it couldn't disguise the strength. There had been times Asher had wondered if it was his earthiness that had drawn her to him. Glimpsing him in a room filled with elegantly attired men and women, she knew it was more than that. It was all of him, every aspect, from temper to humor, that had made her his.

The Wimbledon Ball was as traditional as the tournament. The music, the lights, the people. It was always an evening to remember for its beauty and tastefulness. Asher counted the hours until it would be over. Scolding herself, she tuned back into the conversation of her dance partner. She'd always enjoyed a party, always found pleasure in quiet well-run affairs. But now she wished she and Ty could have shared a bottle of wine in their room.

She didn't want the spotlight this evening, but candlelight. Over the heads of the other dancers her eyes met Ty's. It took only one brief glance to know that his thoughts mirrored hers. Love threatened to drown her.

"You're a lovely dancer, Miss Wolfe."

As the music ended, Asher smiled at her partner. "Thank you." Her smile never wavered as it ran through her head that she had completely forgotten the man's name.

"I was a great fan of your father's, you know." The man cupped a hand under her elbow to lead her from the dance floor. "The Golden Boy of Tennis." With a sigh he patted Asher's hand. "Of course, I remember his early days, before you were born."

"Wimbledon has always been his favorite. Dad loved the tradition . . . and the pomp," Asher added with a smile.

"Seeing the second generation here is good for the soul." In a courtly gesture he lifted her hand to his lips. "My best to you, Miss Wolfe."

"Jerry, how are you?"

A stately woman in silk brocade swept up to them. Lady Mallow, Eric Wickerton's sister, was as always elegant. Asher's spine stiffened.

"Lucy, what a pleasure!"

She offered her fingers to be kissed, sending Asher a brief glance as she did so. "Jerry, Brian's been searching for you to say hello. He's just over there."

"Well then, if you ladies will excuse me."

Having dispatched him, Lucy turned to her former sister-in-law. "Asher, you're looking well."

"Thank you, Lucy."

She gave Asher's simple ivory sheath a brief survey, thinking that if she had worn something so basic, she would have blended in with the wallpaper. On Asher, the muted color and simple lines were stunning. Lucy gave her a candid stare. "And are you well?"

A bit surprised, Asher lifted a brow. "Yes, quite well. And you?"

"I meant that as more than small talk." Lucy's hesitation was brief, as was her glance to determine if they could be overheard. "There's something I've wanted to say to you for a long time." Stiffening, Asher waited. "I love my brother," Lucy began. "I know you didn't. I also know that throughout your marriage you did nothing to disgrace him, though he didn't return the favor."

The unexpected words had Asher staring. "Lucy—"

"Loving him doesn't blind me, Asher," she continued briskly. "My loyalty is with Eric, and always shall be."

"Yes, I understand that."

Lucy studied Asher's face a moment, then she seemed to sigh. "I gave you no support when you were my brother's wife and I wanted to offer my apologies."

Touched, Asher took her hand. "There's no need. Eric and I were simply wrong for each other."

"I often wondered why you married him," Lucy

mused, still searching Asher's face. "At first I thought it was the title, but that had nothing to do with it. Something seemed to change between you so soon after you were married, hardly two months." Asher's eyes clouded for only a moment under Lucy's direct gaze. "I wondered if you'd taken a lover. But it became very obvious in a short time that it was Eric, not you, who was . . . dallying. Just as it's become obvious that there's been only one man in your life." Her gaze shifted. Asher didn't have to follow it to know it rested on Ty.

"Knowing that hurt Eric."

"Knowing that, Eric should never have married you." Lucy sighed again, a bit indulgently. "But then, he's always wanted what belonged to someone else. I won't speak of that, but I'll tell you now what I should have told you long before—I wish you happiness."

On impulse, Asher kissed her cheek. "Thank you, Lucy."

Smiling, she glanced over at Ty again. "Your taste, Asher, has always been exquisite. I've envied it, though it's never been right for me. It's time I joined Brian."

As she turned away, Asher touched her hand. "If I wrote you, would you be uncomfortable?"

"I'd be very pleased." Lucy moved away, silks rustling.

Smiling, Asher realized she had been right. Wimbledon was her turning point. Another layer of guilt had been lifted. She was coming closer to discovering who she was, and what she needed. Feeling a hand on her arm, she turned to smile at Ty.

"Who was that?"

"An old friend." Asher lifted a hand to his cheek. "Dance with me? There's no other way I can hold you until we can be alone."

Chapter Nine

Asher knew she had made great strides when pressure from the press no longer tightened her nerves. Her habitual terror of saying the wrong thing, or saying too much, faded. She still had secrets. Before coming to Australia she'd promised herself a moratorium. Whatever decisions had to be made would wait. For the moment she wanted to concentrate on happiness. Happiness was Ty—and tennis.

There were good memories in Australia—wins, losses. Good tennis. The people were relaxed, casual. The friendliness was exactly what Asher needed after the tension of England. Aussies remembered The Face, and welcomed her. For the first time since her comeback Asher found the winning taking second place to the enjoying.

The change in her was noticeable even during the

early rounds. Her smiles came more frequently. Though her play was no less intense and concentrated, the air of being driven was fading.

From the first row of the stands Ty watched her in early morning practice. He'd just completed two hours of his own. Now, his legs stretched out, he studied her from behind the protection of tinted glasses. She'd improved, he mused . . . not only as an athlete. He remembered how important athletic ability was to her. The fact that she was a strategist and a craftsman had never been enough. Always, she had striven to be recognized as a good athlete. And so she would be, he thought, as she raced to the net to slap a return with her two-fisted backhand. Perhaps in some ways the years of retirement had toughened her.

His face clouded a moment. Consciously he smoothed the frown away. This wasn't the time to think of that or to dwell on the questions that still plagued him. Whys—so many whys hammered at him. Yet he recognized that she was grabbing this time to be carefree. He'd give her that. He would wait. But when the season was over, he'd have his answers.

When her laughter floated to him he forgot the doubts. It was a rich, warm sound, heard all too rarely. Leaning back, Ty chugged down cold fruit juice and looked around him.

If Wimbledon was his favorite stadium, the grass of Kooyong was his favorite surface. It was as hard as a roadbed and fast. A ball bounced true here, unlike other grass courts. Even at the end of the season, when the courts were worn and soiled, the surface remained even. Even after a deluge of rain, the Australian grass was resilient. Kooyong was a treasure for the fast, for the aggressive. Ty was ready for just such a match. Through half-closed eyes he watched Asher. She was ready, too, he decided. And even more ready to enjoy it. A smile touched his mouth. Whatever questions there were, whatever answers, nothing could harm what was between them now.

Noting the practice session was winding up, Ty jumped lightly down to the court. "How about a quick game?"

Madge shot him a look and continued to pack up her rackets. "Forget it, hotshot."

He grabbed a racket from her, bouncing a ball lightly on the strings. "Spot you two points."

With a snort Madge snatched the ball, dropping it into the can. "Take him on, Asher," she suggested. "He needs a lesson."

Catching her tongue between her teeth, Asher studied him. "Head to head," she decided.

"You serve."

Asher waited until he had taken his receiving position. Cupping two balls in her hand, she sent him a smile. "Been a while, hasn't it, Starbuck?"

"Last time we played you never got to game point." He gave Madge a wink. "Sure you don't want that handicap?"

Her ace answered for her. As pleased as he was surprised, Ty sent her a long look. Removing the tinted glasses, he tossed them to Madge. "Not bad, Face." His eyes followed the trail of the next serve. He sent it to the far corner to brush the service line.

Ty liked nothing better than to watch Asher run. The range of her backhand was limited, but perfectly placed. He was on it in a flash. The last time they had played he had beaten her handily even while holding back. Now he scented challenge.

Asher lined the ball straight at him, hard and fast. Pivoting, Ty slammed it back. The ball whistled on her return. With a powerful swing Ty sent her to the baseline, then nipped her return so that the ball brushed the net and died in the forecourt.

"Fifteen–all." Ty feigned a yawn as he went back to position.

Narrowing her eyes, Asher served. The rally was a study in speed and footwork. She knew he was playing with her, moving her all over the court. Aware that she was no match for his power, she chose to catch him off guard. The ball thudded. She raced. It soared. She followed. The sounds of rackets cutting air had a steady, almost musical sound. A rhythm was set. Patiently she adhered to it until she sensed Ty relaxing. Abruptly she altered the pacing and slapped the ball past him.

"Getting crafty," he muttered.

"Getting slow, old timer," she retorted sweetly.

Ty slammed her next serve crosscourt. After the bounce, it landed somewhere in the grandstands. Under her breath Asher swore pungently.

"Did you say something?"

"Not a thing." Disgusted, Asher shook her hair back. As she readied to serve, she caught the look in Ty's eyes. They rested not on her ball or racket, but on her mouth.

All's fair, she mused with a secret smile. Slowly

and deliberately she moistened her lips with the tip of her tongue. Taking a long, preliminary stretch, she served. Distracted, Ty was slow to meet the ball. Asher had little trouble blowing the return past him.

"Game point," she said softly, sending him an intimate smile. Keeping her back to him, she bent to pick up a fresh ball, taking her time about it. She could almost feel Ty's eyes run up the long length of her legs. Smoothing a hand down her hip, she walked back to the baseline. "Ready?"

He nodded, dragging his eyes away from the subtle sweep of her breasts. When his eyes met hers, he read an invitation that had his pulse racing. His concentration broken, he barely returned her serve. The rally was very short.

Victorious, Asher let out a hoot of laughter before she walked to the net. "Your game seemed to be a bit off, Starbuck."

The jibe and the laughter in her eyes had him wanting to strangle her . . . and devour her. "Cheat," he murmured as he walked to meet her at the net.

Asher's look was guileless and she was faintly shocked. "I have no idea what you're talking about." The words were hardly out of her mouth when she was pulled against him, her lips crushed under his. Laughter and desire seemed to bubble in her simultaneously. Without being aware of it, she dropped her racket and clung to him.

"You're lucky I don't toss you on the ground here and now," he mumbled against her mouth.

"What's lucky about that?" Enchanted, Asher

strained against him. How was it possible for one kiss to make her head swim?"

Ty drew back, inches only. His whole body was throbbing for her. "Don't tempt me."

"Do I?" she asked huskily.

"Damn you, Asher. You know just how much."

His voice shook, delighting her. She found she needed him to be as vulnerable as she. "I'm never sure," she whispered, dropping her head to his chest.

His heart was beating too rapidly. Ty tried to fight down the impossible surge of need. Not the time, not the place, his sanity stated. Control was necessary. "You were sure enough to use a few tricks to distract me."

Lifting her head, Asher smiled at him. "Distract you? How?"

"Took your time picking up that ball, didn't you?"

She seemed to consider a moment. "Why, I've seen Chuck do the same thing playing against you. It never seemed to make any difference." She let out a whoop of surprise as he lifted her up and over the net.

"Next time I'll be ready for you, Face." After giving her a brief, bruising kiss, he dropped her to her feet. "You could play naked and I wouldn't blink an eye."

Catching her lip between her teeth, she sent him a teasing glance. "Wanna bet?" Before he could connect his racket with her bottom, she dashed away.

The locker room wasn't empty as Asher walked in, but the crowd was thinning. With the fifth rounds completed, there were fewer contenders, and there-

fore, fewer bodies. She was looking forward to her
match that afternoon with a hot newcomer who had
hopped up in the rankings from one hundred and
twentieth to forty-third in one year. Asher had no
intention of strolling into the finals. Even the pressure of Grand Slam potential couldn't mar her
mood. If ever there was a year she could win it,
Asher felt it was this one.

She greeted a towel-clad Tia Conway as the
Australian emerged from the showers. Both women
knew they would face each other before the tournament was over. Asher could hear a laughing argu-
ment taking place over the sound of running water.
As she started to remove her warm-up jacket, she
spotted Madge in a corner.

The brunette sat with her head leaning back
against the wall, her eyes shut. She was pale despite
her tan, and there were beads of perspiration on her
brow. Asher rushed over to kneel at her feet.

"Madge."

Opening her eyes slowly, Madge sighed. "Who
won?"

For a moment Asher went blank. "Oh, I did. I
cheated."

"Smart girl."

"Madge, what's wrong? God, your hands are like
ice."

"No, it's nothing." She let out a breath as she
leaned forward.

"You're sick, let me—"

"No, I've finished being sick." After a weak smile
Madge swiped the sweat from her brow. "I'll be fine
in a minute."

"You look terrible. You need a doctor." Asher sprang to her feet. "I'll call someone." Before she could move, Madge had her hand.

"I've seen a doctor."

Every sort of nightmare went through Asher's head. In stark terror she stared at her friend. "Oh, God, Madge, how bad?"

"I've got seven months." As Asher swayed, Madge caught her arm tightly. "Good grief, Asher, I'm pregnant, not dying."

Stunned, Asher sank to the bench. *"Pregnant!"*

"Shh." Quickly Madge glanced around. "I'd like to keep this quiet for a while. Damn morning sickness catches me off guard at the worst times." Letting out a shaky breath, she relaxed against the wall again. "The good news is it's not supposed to last long."

"I don't—Madge, I don't know what to say."

"How about congratulations?"

Shaking her head, Asher gripped both of Madge's hands in hers. "Is this what you want?"

"Are you kidding!" On a half laugh, Madge leaned against Asher's shoulder. "I might not look too happy at the moment, but inside I'm doing cartwheels. I've never wanted anything so badly in my life." She sat silently for a moment, her hand still in Asher's. "You know, during my twenties all I could think about was being number one. It was great being there. The Wrightman Cup, Wimbledon, Dallas—all of it. I was twenty-eight when I met The Dean, and still ambitious as hell. I didn't want to get married, but I couldn't live without him. As for kids, I thought, hell, there's plenty of time for that. Later, always later. Well, I woke up one morning in the hospital with my leg screaming at me and I realized I was thirty-two years old. I'd won just about everything I thought I had to win, and yet something was missing. For the better part of my life I've floated around this old world from court to court. Team tennis, pro-am tourneys, celebrity exhibitions, you name it. Until The Dean there was nothing but tennis for me. Even after him, it was the biggest slice of the pie."

"You're a champion," Asher said softly.

"Yeah." Madge laughed again. "Yeah, by God, I am, and I like it. But you know what? When I looked at the snapshot of Ty's nephew I realized that I wanted a baby, The Dean's baby, more than I'd ever wanted a Wimbledon plate. Isn't that wild?"

She let the statement hang in silence a moment as both women absorbed it. "This is going to be my last tournament, and even while that's hurting, I keep wishing it was over so I could go home and start knitting booties."

"You don't know how to knit," Asher murmured.

"Well, The Dean can knit them then. I'll just sit around and get fat." Twisting her head to grin at Asher, Madge saw the tears. "Hey, what's this?"

"I'm happy for you," Asher muttered. She could remember her own feelings on learning of her pregnancy—the fear, the joy, the nausea and elation. She'd wanted to learn to sew. Then it had been over so quickly.

"You look overjoyed," Madge commented, brushing a tear away.

"I am really." She caught Madge to her in a viselike hug. "You'll take care of yourself, won't you? Don't overdo or take any chances?"

"Sure." Something in the tone had the seed of a thought germinating. "Asher, did you . . . Did something happen when you were married to Eric?"

Asher held her tighter for a moment, then released her. "Not now. Maybe someday we'll talk about it. How does The Dean feel about all this?"

Madge gave her a long, measuring look. The non-answer was answer enough, so she let it lay. "He was all set to take out a full-page ad in *World of Sports*," she stated. "I've made him wait until I officially retire."

"There's no need to retire, Madge. You can take a year or two off, lots of women do."

"Not this one." Stretching her arms to the ceiling, Madge grinned. "I'm going out a winner, ranked fifth. When I get home, I'm going to learn how to use a vacuum cleaner."

"I'll believe that when I see it."

"You and Ty are invited to my first home-cooked dinner."

"Great." Asher kissed her cheek. "We'll bring the antacid."

"Not nice," Madge mused. "But wise. Hey, Face," she continued before Asher could rise. "I wouldn't want this to get around but"—her eyes were suddenly very young, and she looked very vulnerable—"I'm scared right out of my socks. I'll be almost thirty-four by the time this kid makes an appearance. I've never even changed a diaper."

Firmly Asher took Madge's shoulders and kissed both of her cheeks. "You're a champion, remember?"

"Yeah, but what do I know about chicken pox?" Madge demanded. "Kids get chicken pox, don't they? And braces, and corrective shoes, and—"

"And mothers who worry before there's anything to worry about," Asher finished. "You're already slipping right into the slot."

"Hey, you're right." Rather pleased with herself, Madge rose. "I'm going to be great."

"You're going to be terrific. Let's get a shower. You've got a doubles match this afternoon."

With feelings mixed and uncertain, Asher rode the elevator to her hotel room late that afternoon. She had won her round with the young upstart from Canada in straight sets. Six–two, six–love. There was little doubt that Asher had played some of the finest tennis in her career in court one. But she didn't think of that now. Her mind kept drifting back to the interlude with Madge, and from there back to her thoughts on learning of her own pregnancy.

Would Ty have wanted to take out full-page ads, or would he have cursed her? Like Eric, would he have accused her of deceit, of trickery? Now that they were being given a second chance, would he want marriage and children? What was it Jess had said that day? she wondered. *Ty will always be a Gypsy, and no woman should ever expect to hold him.*

Yet Asher had expected to hold him, and, despite all her vows, was beginning to expect it again. Her love was so huge, so consuming, that when she was with him, it was simply impossible to conceive of doing without him. And perhaps because she had once, briefly, carried his child inside her, the need to do so again was overwhelming.

Could a woman tame a comet? she asked herself. Should she? For that's what he was—a star that flew, full of speed and light. He wasn't the prince at the end of the fairy tale who would calmly take up his kingdom and sit on a throne. Ty would always search for the next quest. And the next woman? Asher wondered, recalling Jess's words again.

Shaking her head, she told herself to think of today. Today they were together. Only a woman who had lived through change after change, hurt after hurt, could fully appreciate the perfection of a moment. Others might not recognize it, but Asher did. And the moment was hers.

She unlocked the door to their suite and was immediately disappointed. He wasn't there. Even had he been sleeping in the other room, she would have sensed him. The air was never still when Ty was around. Tossing her bag aside, she wandered to the window. The light was still full as the sun had only just began to set. Perhaps they would go out and explore Melbourne, find one of the tiny little clubs with loud music and laughter. She'd like to dance.

Twirling in a circle, Asher laughed. Yes, she would like to dance, to celebrate for Madge . . . and for herself. She was with the man she loved. A bath, she decided. A long, luxurious bath before she changed into something cool and sexy. When she opened the door to the bedroom, Asher stopped and stared in astonishment.

Balloons. Red, yellow, blue, pink and white. They floated throughout the room in a jamboree of color. Helium-filled, they rose to the ceiling, trailing long ribbons. There were dozens of them—round, oval, thin and fat. It was as if a circus had passed hurriedly through, leaving a few souvenirs. Grasping a ribbon, Asher drew one down to her while she continued to stare.

They were three layers deep, she saw in astonishment—at least a hundred of them bumping against one another. Her laughter came out in a quick burst that went on and on.

Who else would think of it? Who else would take the time? Not flowers or jewelry for Ty Starbuck. At that moment she could have floated to the ceiling to join the gift he had given her.

"Hi."

She turned to see him lounging in the doorway. In a flash Asher had launched herself into his arms, the single balloon still grasped in her hand. "Oh, you're crazy!" she cried before she found his lips with hers. With her arms wrapped around his neck, her legs around his waist, she kissed him again and again. "Absolutely insane."

"Me?" he countered. "You're the one standing here surrounded by balloons."

"It's the best surprise I've ever had."

"Better than roses in the bathtub?"

Tossing her head back, she laughed. "Even better than that."

"I thought about diamonds, but they didn't seem like as much fun." As he spoke he moved toward the bed.

"And they don't float," Asher put in, looking up at the ceiling of colorful shapes.

"Good point," Ty conceded as they fell together onto the bed. "Got any ideas how we should spend the evening?"

"One or two," Asher murmured. The balloon she held drifted up to join the others.

"Let's do both." He stopped her laugh with a soft kiss that became hungry quickly. "Oh, God, I've waited all day to be alone with you. When the season's over we'll find someplace—an island, another planet—anyplace where there's no one but us."

"Anyplace," she whispered in agreement while her hands tugged at his shirt.

Passion soared swiftly. Ty's needs doubled as he sensed hers. She was always soft, always eager for him. If the pounding of his blood would have allowed, he would have revered her. But the force of their joined desire wouldn't permit reverence. Clothes were hastily peeled away—a blouse flung aside, a shirt cast to the floor. Overhead, the balloons danced while they savored each other. The scent of victory seemed to cling to both of them, mixed with the faint fragrance of soap and shampoo from the post-game showers. Her lips tasted warm and moist, and somehow of himself as much as of her.

When there was nothing to separate them, they tangled together, their bodies hot and throbbing. With questing hands he moved over territory only more exciting in its familiarity. He could feel reason spin away into pure sensation. Soft here, firm there, her body was endless delight. The warmth of her breath along his skin could make him tremble. Her moan, as he slipped his fingers into her, made him ache. With open-mouthed kisses he trailed over her, seeking the hot heady flavor of her flesh. It seemed to melt into him, filling him to bursting.

When she arched, offering everything, Ty felt a surge of power so awesome he almost feared to take her. Too strong, he thought hazily. He was too strong and was bound to hurt her. He felt he could have lifted the world without effort. Yet she was drawing him to her with murmuring pleas.

There was no control in madness. She stole his sanity with her smooth skin and soft lips. There were no more pastel colors from frivolous balloons. Now there was gleaming silver and molten reds and pulsing blacks whirling and churning into a wild kaleidoscope that seemed to pull him into its vortex. Gasping her name, Ty thrust into her. The colors shattered, seeming to pierce his skin with a multitude of shards. And in the pain was indescribable pleasure.

When he was spent, nestled between her breasts, Asher gazed up at the darkening ceiling. How could it be, she wondered, that each time they were together it was different? Sometimes they loved in laughter, sometimes in tenderness. At other times with a smoldering passion. This time there had been a taste of madness in their loving. Did other lovers find this infinite variety, this insatiable delight in each other? Perhaps the two of them were unique. The thought was almost frightening.

"What are you thinking?" Ty asked. He knew he should shift his weight from her, but found no energy to do so.

"I was wondering if it should be so special each time I'm with you."

He laughed, kissing the side of her breast. "Of course it should, I'm a special person. Don't you read the sports section?"

She tugged his hair, but tenderly. "Don't let your press go to your head, Starbuck. You have to win a few more matches before you wrap up the Grand Slam."

He massaged the muscles of her thigh. "So do you, Face."

"I'm only thinking as far ahead as the next game," she said. She didn't want to think of Forest Hills, or the States—or the end of the season. "Madge is pregnant," she said half to herself.

"What!" Like a shot, Ty's head came up.

"Madge is pregnant," Asher repeated. "She wants to keep it quiet until the Australian Open is over."

"I'll be damned," he exclaimed. "Old Madge."

"She's only a year older than you," Asher stated defensively, causing him to laugh again.

"It's an expression, love." Absently he twined one of Asher's curls around a finger. "How does she feel about it?"

"She's thrilled—and scared." Her lashes lowered, shielding her expression a moment. "She's going to retire."

"We're going to have to throw her one hell of a

party." Rolling onto his back, he drew Asher close to his side.

After a moment she moistened her lips and spoke casually. "Do you ever think about children? I mean, it would be difficult, wouldn't it, combining a family with a profession like this?"

"It's done all the time, depends on how you go about it."

"Yes, but all the traveling, the pressure."

He started to pass it off, then remembered how she had lived her childhood. Though he had never sensed any resentment in her, he wondered if she felt a family would be a hindrance to her career. Physically a baby would prevent her from playing for some time. And she'd already lost three years, he reflected with an inner sigh. Ty pushed the idea of their children out of his mind. There was time, after all.

"I imagine it's a hassle to worry about kids when you've got a tournament to think of," he said lightly. "A player's got enough trouble keeping track of his rackets."

With a murmured agreement, Asher stared into space.

In the thin light of dawn she shifted, brushing at a tickle on her arm. Something brushed over her cheek. Annoyed, Asher lifted her hand to knock it away. It came back. With a softly uttered complaint she opened her eyes.

In the gray light she could see dozens of shapes. Some hung halfway to the ceiling, others littered the bed and floor. Sleepy, she stared at them without comprehension. Irritated at having been disturbed, she knocked at the shape that rested on her hip. It floated lazily away.

Balloons, she realized. Turning her head, she saw that Ty was all but buried under them. She chuckled, muffling the sound with her hand as she sat up. He lay flat on his stomach, facedown in the pillow. She plucked a red balloon from the back of his head. He didn't budge. Leaning over, she outlined his ear with kisses. He muttered and stirred and shifted away. Asher lifted a brow. A challenge, she decided.

After brushing the hair from the nape of his neck, she began to nibble on the exposed flesh. "Ty," she whispered. "We have company."

Feeling a prickle of drowsy pleasure, Ty rolled to his side, reaching for her. Asher placed a balloon in his hand. Unfocused, his eyes opened.

"What the hell is this?"

"We're surrounded," Asher told him in a whisper. "They're everywhere."

A half dozen balloons tipped to the floor as he shifted to his back. After rubbing his face with his hands, he stared. "Good God." With that he shut his eyes again.

Not to be discouraged, Asher straddled him. "Ty, it's morning."

"Uh-uh."

"I have that talk show to do at nine."

He yawned and patted her bottom. "Good luck."

She planted a soft, nibbling kiss on his lips. "I have two hours before I have to leave."

" 'S okay, you won't bother me."

Wanna bet? she asked silently. Reaching out, she trailed her fingers up his thigh. "Maybe I'll sleep a bit longer."

"Mmm-hmm."

Slowly she lay on top of him, nuzzling her lips at her throat. "I'm not bothering you, am I?"

"Hmm?"

She snuggled closer, feeling her breasts rub against his soft mat of hair. "Cold," she mumbled, and moved her thigh against his.

"Turn down the air conditioning," Ty suggested.

Brows lowered, Asher lifted her head. Ty's eyes met hers, laughing, and not a bit sleepy. With a toss of her head Asher rolled from him and tugged on the blanket. Though her back was to him, she could all but see his grin.

"How's this?" Wrapping an arm around her waist, he fit his body to hers. She gave him a shrug as an answer. "Warmer?" he asked as he slid his hand up to cup her breast. The point was already taut, her pulse already racing. Ty moved sinuously against her.

"The air conditioning's too high," she said plaintively. "I'm freezing."

Ty dropped a kiss at the base of her neck. "I'll get it." He rose, moving to the unit. It shut off with a dull mechanical thud. With a teasing remark on the tip of his tongue, he turned.

In the fragile morning light she lay naked in the tumbled bed, surrounded by gay balloons. Her hair rioted around a face dominated by dark, sleepy eyes. The faintest of smiles touched her lips, knowing, inviting, challenging. All thoughts of joking left him. Her skin was so smooth and touched with gold. Like a fist in the solar plexus, desire struck him and stole his breath.

As he went to her, Asher lifted her arms to welcome him.

Chapter Ten

*A*sher, how does it feel being only three matches away from the Grand Slam?"

"I'm trying not to think about it."

"You've drawn Stacie Kingston in the quarterfinals. She's got an oh-for-five record against you. Does that boost your confidence?"

"Stacie's a strong player, and very tough. I'd never go into a match with her overconfident."

Her hands folded loosely, Asher sat behind the table facing the lights and reporters. The microphone in front of her picked up her calm, steady voice and carried it to the rear of the room. She wore her old team tennis jacket with loose warm-up pants and court shoes. Around her face her hair curled damply. They'd barely given her time to shower after her most recent win at Forest Hills before scheduling the impromptu press conference. The cameras were rolling, taping her every movement, recording every expression. One of the print reporters quickly scribbled down that she wore no jewelry or lipstick.

"Did you expect your comeback to be this successful?"

Asher gave a lightning-fast grin—here then gone —something she would never have done for the press even two months before. "I trained hard," she said simply.

"Do you still lift weights?"

"Every day."

"Have you changed your style this time around?"

"I think I've tightened a few things up." She relaxed, considering. Of all the people in the room, only Asher was aware that her outlook toward the press had changed. There was no tightness in her throat as she spoke. No warning signals to take care flashed in her brain. "Improved my serve particularly," she continued. "My percentage of aces and service winners is much higher than it was three or four years ago."

"How often did you play during your retirement?"

"Not often enough."

"Will your father be coaching you again?"

Her hesitation was almost too brief to be measured. "Not officially," she replied evasively.

"Have you decided to accept the offer of a layout in *Elegance* magazine?"

Asher tucked a lock of hair behind her ear. "News

travels fast." Laughter scattered around the room. "I haven't really decided," she continued. "At the moment I'm more concerned with the U.S. Open."

"Who do you pick to be your opponent in the finals?"

"I'd like to get through the quarters and semis first."

"Let's say, who do you think will be your strongest competition?"

"Tia Conway," Asher answered immediately. Their duel in Kooyong was still fresh in her mind. Three exhausting sets—three tie breakers—in two grueling hours. "She's the best all-around woman player today."

"What makes you say that?"

"Tia has court sense, speed, strength and a big serve."

"Yet you've beaten her consistently this season."

"But not easily."

"What about the men's competition? Would you predict the U.S. will have two Grand Slam winners this year?"

Asher fielded the question first with a smile. "I think someone mentioned that there were still three matches to go, but I believe it's safe to say that if Starbuck continues to play as he's played all season, no one will beat him, particularly on grass, as it's his best surface."

"Is your opinion influenced by personal feelings?"

"Statistics don't have any feelings," she countered. "Personal or otherwise." Asher rose, effectively curtailing further questioning. A few more were tossed out at random, but she merely leaned toward the mike and apologized for having to end the meeting. As she started to slip through a rear door, she spotted Chuck.

"Nicely done, Face."

"And over," she breathed. "What are you doing here?"

"Keeping an eye on my best friend's lady," he said glibly as he slipped an arm around her shoulders. "Ty thought it would be less confusing if he kept out of the way during your little tête-à-tête with the members of the working press."

"For heaven's sake," Asher mumbled, "I don't need a keeper."

"Don't tell me." Chuck flashed his boy-next-door smile. "Ty had it in his head the press might badger you."

Tilting her head, Asher studied his deceptively sweet face. "And what were you going to do if they had?"

"Strong-arm 'em," he claimed while flexing his muscle. "Though I might have been tempted to let them take a few bites out of you after that comment about nobody beating Ty. Didn't you hear they were naming a racket after me?"

Asher circled his waist with her arm. "Sorry, friend, I call 'em like I see 'em."

Stopping, he put both hands on Asher's shoulders and studied her. His look remained serious even when she gave him a quizzical smile. "You know, Face, you really look good."

She laughed. "Well, thanks . . . I think. Did I look bad before?"

"I don't mean you look beautiful, that never changes. I mean you look happy."

Lifting a hand to the one on her shoulder, Asher squeezed. "I am happy."

"It shows. In Ty too." Briefly he hesitated, then plunged ahead. "Listen, I don't know what happened between you two before, but—"

"Chuck . . ." Asher shook her head to ward off questions.

"But," he continued, "I want you to know I hope you make it this time."

"Oh, Chuck." Shutting her eyes, she went into his arms. "So do I," she sighed. "So do I."

"I asked you to keep an eye on her," Ty said from behind them. "I didn't say anything about touching."

"Oh, hell." Chuck tightened his hold. "Don't be so selfish. Second-seeds need love too." Glancing down at Asher, he grinned. "Can I interest you in lobster tails and champagne?"

"Sorry." She kissed his nose. "Somebody already offered me pizza and cheap wine."

"Outclassed again." With a sigh Chuck released her. "I need somebody to hit with tomorrow," he told Ty.

"Okay."

"Six o'clock, court three."

"You buy the coffee."

"We'll flip for it," Chuck countered before he sauntered away.

Alone, Asher and Ty stood for a moment in awkward silence while an airplane droned by over-

head. The awkwardness had cropped up occasionally on their return to the States. It was always brief
and never commented on. In the few seconds without words, each of them admitted that full truths
would soon be necessary. Neither of them knew how
to approach it.

"So," Ty began as the moment passed, "how did it
go?"

"Easily," Asher returned, smiling as she stood on
tiptoe to kiss him. "I didn't need the bodyguard."

"I know how you feel about press conferences."

"How?"

"Oh . . ." He combed her hair with his fingers.
"Terrified's a good word."

With a laugh she held out her hand as they started
to walk. *"Was* a good word," Asher corrected him.
"I'm amazed I ever let it get to me. There was one
problem though."

"What?"

"I was afraid I'd faint from starvation." She sent
him a pitiful look from under her lashes. "Someone
did mention pizza, didn't they?"

"Yeah." He grinned, catching her close. "And
cheap wine."

"You really know how to treat a woman, Starbuck," Asher told him in a breathless whisper.

"We'll go Dutch," he added before he pulled her
toward the car.

Twenty minutes later they sat together at a tiny
round table. There was the scent of rich sauce, spice
and melted candles. From the jukebox in the corner
poured an endless succession of popular rock tunes

at a volume just below blaring. The waitresses wore bib aprons sporting pictures of grinning pizzas. Leaning her elbows on the scarred wooden table, Asher stared soulfully into Ty's eyes.

"You know how to pick a class joint, don't you?"

"Stick with me, Face," he advised. "I've got a hamburger palace picked out for tomorrow. You get your own individual plastic packs of catsup." Her lips curved up, making him want to taste them. Leaning forward, he did. The table tilted dangerously.

"You two ready to order?" Snapping her wad of gum, the waitress shifted her weight to one hip.

"Pizza and a bottle of Chianti," Ty told her, kissing Asher again.

"Small, medium or large?"

"Small, medium or large what?"

"Pizza," the waitress said with exaggerated patience.

"Medium ought to do it." Twisting his head, Ty sent the waitress a smile that had her pulling back her shoulders. "Thanks."

"Well, that should improve the service," Asher considered as she watched the woman saunter away.

"What's that?"

Asher studied his laughing eyes. "Never mind," she decided. "Your ego doesn't need any oiling."

Ty bent his head closer to hers as a defense against the jukebox. "So what kind of questions did they toss at you?"

"The usual. They mentioned the business from *Elegance.*"

"Are you going to do it?"

She moved her shoulders. "I don't know. It might be fun. And I don't suppose it would hurt the image of women's tennis for one of the players to be in a national fashion magazine."

"It's been done before."

Asher conquered a grin and arched her brows instead. "Do you read fashion magazines, Starbuck?"

"Sure. I like to look at pretty women."

"I always thought jocks tended to favor other sorts of magazines for that."

He gave her an innocent look. "What sorts of magazines?"

Ignoring him, Asher went back to his original question. "They're playing up this Grand Slam business for all it's worth."

"Bother you?" As he laced their fingers together, he studied them. There was an almost stunning difference in size and texture. Often he'd wondered how such an elegant little hand could be so strong . . . and why it should fit so perfectly with his.

"A bit," Asher admitted, enjoying the rough feel of his skin against hers. "It makes it difficult to go into a match thinking of just that match. What about you? I know you're getting the same kind of pressure."

The waitress brought the wine, giving Ty a slow smile as she set down the glasses. To Asher's amusement, he returned it. He's a devil, she thought. And he knows it.

"I always look at playing a game at a time, one

point at a time." He poured a generous amount of wine in both glasses. "Three matches is a hell of a lot of points."

"But you'd like to win the Grand Slam?"

Raising his glass, he grinned. "Damn right." He laughed into her eyes as he drank. "Of course, Martin's already making book on it."

"I'm surprised he's not here," Asher commented, "analyzing every volley."

"He's coming in tomorrow with the rest of the family."

Asher's fingers tightened on the stem of her glass. "The rest of the family?"

"Yeah, Mom and Jess for sure. Mac and Pete if it can be arranged." The Chianti was heavy and mellow. Ty relaxed with it. "You'll like Pete; he's a cute kid."

She mumbled something into her wine before she swallowed. Martin had been there three years ago, along with Ty's mother and sister. Both she and Ty had gone into the U.S. Open as top seeds; both had been hounded by the press. The two of them had shared meals then, too, and a bed. So much was the same—terrifyingly so. But there had been so much in between.

There'd been no small boy with Ty's coloring then. No small boy with that air of perpetual energy to remind her of what was lost. Asher felt the emptiness inside her, then the ache, as she did each time she thought of the child.

Misinterpreting her silence, Ty reached over to take her hand. "Asher, you still haven't spoken to your father?"

"What?" Disoriented, she stared at him a moment. "No, no, not since . . . Not since I retired."

"Why don't you call him?"

"I can't."

"That's ridiculous. He's your father."

She sighed, wishing it were so simple. "Ty, you know him. He's a very stringent man, very certain of what's right and what's wrong. When I left tennis I did more than disappoint him, I . . . wasted what he'd given me."

Ty answered with a short, explicit word that made her smile. "From his viewpoint that's the way it was," she went on. "As Jim Wolfe's daughter I had certain responsibilities. In marrying Eric and giving up my career I shirked them. He hasn't forgiven me."

"How do you know that?" he demanded. His voice was low under the insistent music, but rich with annoyance. "If you haven't spoken to him, how can you be sure how he feels now?"

"Ty, if his feelings had changed, wouldn't he be here?" She shrugged, wishing they could have avoided the subject for a while longer. "I thought, at first, that when I started playing again it might make the difference. It hasn't."

"But you miss him."

Even that wasn't so simple. To Ty, family meant something warm and loving and eternal. He'd never understand that Asher looked not so much now for her father's presence or even his love, but simply his forgiveness. "I'd like him to be here," she said finally. "But I understand his reasons for not coming." Her brow clouded for a moment with a realization that had just come to her. "Before, I played for him, to please him, to justify the time and effort he put into my career. Now I play for myself."

"And you play better," Ty put in. "Perhaps that's one of the reasons."

With a smile she lifted his hand to her lips. "Perhaps that's one of them."

"Here's your pizza." The waitress plopped the steaming pan between them.

They ate amid noise and their own casual chatter. Even the pressure of the upcoming matches had no effect on Asher's mood. The cheese was hot and stringy, making Ty laugh as she struggled against it. The contents of the squat bottle of Chianti lowered as they drank leisurely, content to let the meal drag on. Tennis was forgotten while they spoke of everything and nothing at all. A group of teenagers poured in, laughing and rowdy, to feed another succession of quarters into the jukebox.

Why am I so happy to be in this loud, crowded room? she wondered. The cooling pizza and lukewarm wine were as appealing as the champagne and caviar they had shared in Paris. It was Ty. The place never mattered when she was with him. Abruptly it occurred to Asher that it was herself as well. She was being herself. There weren't any guards, or the need for any. Ty was the only man she'd ever been close to who required none from her.

Her father had wanted her to be perfect—his glass princess. All through her youth she had done everything in her power to please him. With Eric, she had been expected to be the cool, well-mannered Lady

Wickerton, a woman who could discuss art and politics intelligently. She was to have been like crystal, many-faceted, elegant and cold.

All Ty had ever expected her to be was Asher. He accepted her flaws, even admired them. Because he had wanted her to be herself, she'd been able to be just that. Not once in all the time she had known him had he ever demanded that she fit a pattern or requested that she conform to any standards but her own. Impulsively she reached over to take his hand, then pressed it to her cheek. There was warmth against warmth, flesh against flesh.

"What's this for?" he asked, allowing his fingers to spread.

"For not wanting glass."

His brows drew together in confusion. "Am I supposed to know what that means?"

"No." Laughing, Asher leaned closer. "Have you drunk enough wine that your resistance is down and you'll be easily seduced?"

A slow smile spread. "More than enough."

"Then come with me," Asher ordered.

It was late when Ty lay sleepless beside Asher. Curled close, her hand caught loosely in his, she slept deeply, drugged with loving and fatigue. Her scent hung in the air so that even in the dark Ty could visualize her. A small alarm clock ticked monotonously at his left, its luminous dial glowing. Twelve twenty-seven.

His mind was far too active for sleep. He sensed, as he knew Asher did, that the idyll was nearly over.

They were back where they had once ended, and questions would not be put off too much longer. Impatience gnawed at him. Unlike Asher, Ty looked for the end of the season. Only then would the time be right for answers and explanations. He was not used to biding his time, and the strain was beginning to tell. Even tonight under the laughter he had understood her wordless request that he not probe.

The question of her father, Ty mused, shifting the pillow to brace his back. She was more unhappy about the estrangement than she admitted. It showed in her eyes. It was incomprehensible to him that members of a family could turn away from one another. His thoughts drifted to his mother, to Jess. There was nothing either of them could do he wouldn't forgive. He'd never be able to bear the thought of being responsible for their unhappiness. Could a father feel any different about a daughter? An only daughter, a much-loved daughter, Ty reflected.

He could remember Jim Wolfe's pride in Asher. Ty had often sat beside him during one of Asher's matches in her early days as a pro, then consistently during her last year. Even in such a private man the adoration had showed. It wasn't possible to believe it had been only for the athlete and not for the woman.

Surprisingly Jim had accepted Ty's relationship with his daughter. No, Ty corrected, approved. He'd seemed to enjoy seeing them together. Once, Ty recalled, he had gone as far as outlining his expectations to Ty of their future. At the time Ty had been both amused and annoyed at the fatherly interference. What plans he had had for a future with Asher had still been vague. Then, when they had crystallized in his mind, it had been too late. Frowning, Ty glanced down at her.

In the pale shaft of moonlight her face seemed very fragile. Her hair was a silvery, insubstantial cloud around it. A wave of longing swamped him so that he had to fight the need to wake her and satisfy himself that she was there for him. His feelings for her had always been mixed—wild desire, unbearable tenderness, traces of fear. There had been no other woman who had ever brought him such sharp and conflicting emotions. Watching her sleep, he felt the need to protect. There should be no shadow of unhappiness in her eyes when they opened.

How many obstacles would they have to overcome before they were really together? he wondered. There was one he might remove himself. Perhaps the time had come to take the first step. On impulse, Ty slipped from the bed and into the sitting room.

It took only moments by phone to travel from coast to coast. Dropping into a chair, Ty listened to the faint crackling on the wire before it began to ring.

"Wolfe residence."

In the two words, Ty recognized the trained voice of a servant. "Jim Wolfe please. It's Ty Starbuck."

"One moment please."

Ty sat back, keeping one ear trained on the adjoining bedroom. He heard two distinct clicks as one extension was lifted and the other replaced.

"Starbuck."

The quiet, cautious voice was instantly recognizable. "Jim. How are you?"

"Well." A bit surprised by the late night call, Jim Wolfe settled behind his desk. "I've been reading quite a bit about you."

"It's been a good year. You were missed at Wimbledon."

"That makes five for you there."

"And three for Asher," he returned pointedly.

There was a moment of complete silence. "Your slice volley's cleaner than it once was."

"Jim, I called to talk about Asher."

"Then we have nothing to say."

For a moment the cool, calm statement left Ty speechless. In a flood, fury took over. "Just a damn minute. I have plenty to say. Your daughter's battled her way back to the top. She's done it without you."

"I'm aware of that. Do you have a point?"

"Yes, I have a point," Ty retorted. "I've never seen anyone work as hard as she has these past few months. And it hasn't been easy, dealing with the pressure, the press, the constant questions on why her father isn't in the stands while she wins championship after championship."

"Asher knows my feelings," Jim said flatly. "They're no concern of yours."

"Whatever concerns Asher concerns me."

"So . . ." Jim picked up a slim gold pen from the desk and carefully examined it. "We're back to that."

"Yes, we are."

"If you've decided to resume your relationship

with Asher, it's your business, Ty." He flung the pen back onto the desk. "And it's my business if I don't."

"For God's sake, Jim," Ty began heatedly, "she's your daughter. You can't turn your back on your own child."

"Like father, like daughter," Jim murmured.

"What the hell does that mean?" Frustrated, Ty rose to pace, dragging the phone with him.

"Asher wiped her child out of existence. I've done the same."

All movement stopped. Ty felt something freeze in him as his knuckles turned white on the receiver. "What child?"

"She turned her back on everything I taught her," Jim went on, not hearing Ty's harshly whispered question. "The daughter I knew couldn't have done it." The words, and the anger that accompanied them, had been held in for years. Now they came bursting out. "I tried to understand why she married that pale excuse for a man, even tried to resign myself to her throwing away her career. But some things I won't forgive. If the life she chose to live was worth the price of my grandchild, she's welcome to it."

Enraged at letting his feelings pour out so openly, Jim slammed down the receiver.

Three thousand miles away Ty stood, staring at nothing. With infinite care he placed the phone back on the table. Too many thoughts were whirling in his head, too many questions and half-answers. He had to think, to take his time. Silently he walked back into the bedroom and dressed.

He wanted to shake her awake and demand an explanation; he wanted to wait until he had a grip on himself. Torn, Ty sat on a chair and stared at the still form in the bed. Asher slept so peacefully, her quiet breathing hardly stirred the air.

A child? Asher's child? But there was no child, Ty reasoned. If Lord and Lady Wickerton had produced an offspring, there would have been some mention of it in the press. An heir was never kept secret. Dragging a hand through his hair, Ty shifted. Besides, he reasoned, if Asher had had a child, where was it? Struggling to overcome the jealousy at imagining Asher's bearing another man's child, Ty went over his conversation with Jim Wolfe again.

Asher wiped her child out of existence. . . .

His fingers tightened on the arms of the chair as he stared at her sleeping form. Abortion? Without warning, a storm of emotion took over that he had to systematically fight back until his pulse leveled. All attempts to think of the word with an open mind were futile. He couldn't rationalize it, not when it was Asher, not when the child was part of her. Could the woman he thought he knew have made that kind of choice? For what purpose? Was it possible that the social life she had sought had been more important than . . .

As bitterness filled him, Ty shook his head. He wouldn't believe it of her. Controlled, yes. There were times Asher could be infuriatingly controlled. But never calculating. Jim had been talking in riddles, he decided. There'd never been a child. There couldn't have been.

He watched Asher stir. With a soft murmur she

shifted toward the emptiness beside her where Ty should have been. He sensed the moment she woke.

The moonlight gleamed on her arm as she lifted it, brushing her fingers at the hair that curled around her face. She placed her hand on his pillow, as if testing it for warmth.

"Ty?"

Not trusting himself, he said nothing. If only she would go back to sleep until he had resolved his feelings. He could still taste the bitterness at the back of his throat.

But she wouldn't sleep. Although groggy, Asher sensed tension in the air. Ty's emotions were always volatile enough to be felt tangibly. *Something's wrong, something's wrong,* hammered in her brain.

"Ty?" she called again, and a hint of fear touched the word. Asher had struggled to a sitting position before she saw him. The moonlight was enough to allow her to see that his eyes were dark and fixed on her face. It was also enough to let her see that they were cold. Her pulse began to race. "Couldn't you sleep?" she asked, struggling to convince herself it was all her imagination.

"No."

Asher laced her fingers together as she swallowed. "You should have woke me."

"Why?"

"We—we could have talked."

"Could we?" Cold anger filled him. "We can talk as long as I don't ask any questions you don't want to answer."

She'd been expecting the showdown, but not like this. His resentment was already wrapping around her. Still, he had a right, and she'd put him off too long. "Ty, if it's answers you want, I'll give them to you."

"Just like that?" he snapped, rising. "Just ask and you'll answer. Nothing more to hide, Asher?"

Stung by his tone, she stared up at him. "It wasn't a matter of hiding, Ty, not really. I needed time—we needed time."

"Why was that, Asher?" he asked in a tone that was uncharacteristically cool. She felt a shudder zip down her spine. "Why was time so important?"

"There were things I wasn't sure you'd understand."

"Like the baby?"

If he had slapped her, Asher couldn't have been more stunned. Even in the moonlight he could see her face go white. Her eyes grew huge and dark and desperate. "How . . ." The words wouldn't form. Though they raced around in her mind, Asher seemed incapable of forcing any through her lips. How had he found out? Who had told him? How long had he known?

"Eric," she managed, though the name threatened to strangle her. "Eric told you."

Sharp disappointment cut through him. Somehow he had hoped it hadn't been true that she had conceived and rejected another man's child. "So it's true," he exclaimed. Turning from her, Ty stared through the window at the darkness. He found he couldn't be logical or objective. It was one thing to understand the concept of freedom of choice, and another to apply it to Asher.

"Ty, I . . ." She tried to speak. All of her worst

fears were hurtling down on her. The gulf between them was already tangible and threatening to widen. If only she had been able to tell him in her own way, in her own time. "Ty, I wanted to tell you myself. There were reasons why I didn't at first, and then . . ." Asher shut her eyes. "Then I made excuses."

"I suppose you thought it was none of my business."

Her eyes flew open again. "How can you say that?"

"What you do with your life when you're married to one man isn't the concern of another, even when he loves you."

Simultaneous flashes of pain and joy rushed through her. "You didn't," she whispered.

"Didn't what?"

"You didn't love me."

He gave a brief laugh, but didn't turn back to her. "No, of course I didn't. That's why I couldn't stay away from you. That's why I thought of you every waking moment."

Asher pressed the heel of her hand between her eyes. Why now? she thought wildly. Why is it all happening now? "You never told me."

This time he turned. "Yes, I did."

Furiously she shook her head. "You never said it. Not once. Even once would have been enough."

In concentration, his brows drew together. She was right, he decided. He'd never said the words. He'd shown her in every way he knew how, but he'd never said the words. "Neither did you," he blurted, speaking his thoughts.

She let out a breath that was perilously close to a sob. "I was afraid to."

"Damn it, Asher, so was I."

For a long, tense moment they stared at each other. Had she been that blind? Had she needed words so badly that she hadn't seen what he'd been giving her? The words would never have come easily to him because they meant everything. For Ty, a declaration of love wasn't a casual phrase but a declaration of self.

Asher swallowed a tremor, wanting her voice to be strong. "I love you, Ty. I've always loved you. And I'm still afraid." As she held out a hand he glanced down at it, but made no move to accept it. "Don't turn away from me now." She thought of the child she had lost. "Please, don't hate me for what I did."

He couldn't understand, but he could feel. It seemed love for her justified anything. Crossing to her, Ty took the offered hand and brought it to his lips. "It'll be better when we've talked this out. We need to start clean, Asher."

"Yes." She closed her hand over their joined ones. "I want that too. Oh, Ty, I'm so sorry about the baby." Her free arm wrapped around his waist as she dropped her head on his chest. The relief, she thought. The relief of at last being able to share it with him. "I couldn't tell you before, when it happened. I didn't know what to do. I didn't know how you'd feel."

"I don't know either," he answered.

"I felt so guilty." She shut her eyes tight. "When

Jess showed me that picture of your nephew, I could almost see how the baby would have looked. I always knew he would have had your hair, your eyes."

"Mine?" For a moment nothing seemed to function. His mind, his heart, his lungs. Then, in a torrent, everything came together. *"Mine?"* Asher gave an involuntary cry as he crushed her fingers in his. Before she could speak he had her by the shoulders, digging into her flesh. His eyes alone brought her ice-cold terror. "The baby was mine?"

Her mouth moved to form words, but nothing came out. Confusion and fear overtook her. But he'd already known, she thought desperately. No, no, he hadn't. Eric's baby, her mind flashed. He'd thought it was Eric's baby.

"Answer me, damn you!" He was shaking her now, violently. Limp as a rag doll, Asher made no protest and sought no defense. Both would have been futile. "Was it my baby? Was it mine?"

She nodded, too numb to feel the pain.

He wanted to strike her. Looking at her face, Ty could almost feel the sensation of his hand stinging against it. And he'd want to keep striking her until rage and grief could no longer be felt. Reading his thoughts in his eyes, Asher made no move to protect herself. For an instant his fingers tightened on her arms. With a violent oath he hurled her away. Hardly daring to breathe, she lay on the bed and waited.

"You bitch. You had my child in you when you married him." He flung the words at her, struggling not to use his fists. "Did he make you get rid of it when he found out? Or did you take care of it so you could play the lady without encumbrances?"

She wasn't aware that her breathing was ragged, or that she was trembling. Her mind was too numb to take in more than half of his words. All she understood was the fury of his feelings. "I didn't know. I didn't know I was pregnant when I married Eric."

"You had no right to keep this from me." Towering over her, he reached down to yank her to her knees. "You had no right to make a decision like that when the child was mine!"

"Ty—"

"Shut up. Damn you!" He shoved her away, knowing neither of them was safe if they remained together. "There's nothing you can say, nothing that could make me even want to look at you again."

He strode from the room without a second glance. The sound of the slamming door echoed over and over in Asher's mind.

Chapter Eleven

$\mathscr{T}$y took the quarter-finals in straight sets. Most said he played the finest tennis in his career on that hazy September afternoon. Ty knew he wasn't playing tennis. He was waging war. He'd gone onto the court full of vengeance and fury, almost pummeling his opponent with the ball. His swing was vicious, his aim deadly.

The violence showed in his face, in the grim set of his mouth, in the eyes that were nearly black with emotion. It wasn't the winning or losing that mattered to him, but the release of the physical aspect of the temper that he'd barely controlled the night before. When he struck, he struck brutally, always moving. The motion itself was a threat. He'd often been called a warrior, but the description had never been more true. As if scenting blood, he hounded his opponent, then ground him mercilessly into the ground.

Ty's only disappointment was that the match didn't last longer. There hadn't been enough time to sweat out all of his fury. He wondered if there would ever be enough time.

In the stands there were differing reactions as he stalked off the courts.

"Name of God, Ada, I've never seen the boy play better." Martin Derick beamed like a new father. His voice was hoarse from cheering and cigarettes. A pile of butts lay crushed at his feet. "Did you see how he massacred that Italian?"

"Yes."

"Oh-ho, two matches more and our boy's going to have a Grand Slam." Martin squeezed Ada's work-worn hands between his two smooth ones. "Nothing's going to stop him now!"

In her quiet, steady way, Ada stared down at the court. She'd seen more than Ty's victory. There'd been fury in her son's eyes. Outrage, hurt. She recognized the combination too well. She'd seen it in a little boy who'd been teased because his father had deserted him. Then, he'd used his fists to compensate. Today, Ada mused, he'd used a racket. As Martin recounted every serve and smash, Ada sat silently and wondered what had put that look back in her son's eyes.

"Mom." Jess leaned close so that her voice wouldn't carry. "Something's wrong with Ty, isn't it?"

"I'd say something's very wrong with Ty."

Jess rubbed her cheek against Pete's, wishing his powdery scent would calm her. Giggling, he squirmed out of her arms and dove toward his father. "Asher wasn't in the stands today."

Ada lifted her eyes to her daughter's. Jess had mentioned, perhaps too casually, that Ty was seeing Asher Wolfe again. Ada had hardly needed the information. Once she had heard Asher was competing again, she'd known what the results would be.

The only time she had ever seen Ty truly devastated had been when Asher had married the polished British lord. His rage and threats had been expected. But they had turned to a brooding that had concerned her a great deal more.

"Yes, I noticed," Ada replied. "Then, she's got a match of her own."

"On the next court, and not for a half hour." Jess cast another worried glance around at the people who filled the stands. "She should have been here."

"Since she wasn't, there must be a reason."

A fresh tremor of unease ran up Jess's back. "Mom, I've got to talk to you—alone. Can we go get a cup of coffee?"

Without question, Ada rose. "You fellas keep Pete entertained," she ordered, tousling her grandson's hair. "Jess and I'll be back in a few minutes."

"You're going to tell her?" Mac spoke softly as he touched his wife's hand.

"Yes. Yes, I need to."

Bouncing his son on his knee, he watched them melt into the crowd.

After they had settled at a table, Ada waited for

her daughter to begin. She knew Jess was marking time, ordering coffee, speculating on the chances of rain. Ada let her ramble. An orderly, even-tempered woman, she had learned the best way to deal with her emotional offsprings was to ride out the storm. Eventually Jess stopped stirring her coffee and lifted her eyes to her mother's.

"Mom, do you remember when we were here three years ago?"

How could she forget? Ada thought with a sigh. That was the year Ty had won the U.S. Open, then barely had time to savor it before the world had crumbled around his ears. "Yes, I remember."

"Asher left Ty and married Eric Wickerton." When Ada remained silent, Jess lifted her coffee cup and drank as if to fortify herself. "It was my fault," she blurted out.

Ada took the time to taste her own coffee, deciding it wasn't half bad for restaurant brew. "Your fault, Jessie? How?"

"I went to see her." In quick jerks Jess began to shred her napkin. She'd thought it would be easier now that she had told Mac everything, but with her mother's gaze steady and patient on hers, she felt like a child again. "I went to her hotel room when I knew Ty wouldn't be there." After pressing her lips together, she let the confession come out in a burst. "I told her Ty was tired of her. I told her he—he was bored."

"I'm surprised she didn't laugh in your face," Ada commented.

Quickly Jess shook her head. "I was convincing,"

she went on. "Maybe because I was convinced it was the truth. And I—I was sympathetic." Remembering how well she had played the role of reluctant messenger tore at her. "Oh, God, Mom, when I look back and remember the things I told her, how I said them . . ." Anguished, her eyes met her mother's. "I told her Ty thought she and Eric were suited to each other. There was enough truth in that, but I turned it around to give her the impression that Ty was hoping Eric would take her off his hands. And I defended Ty, telling Asher he'd never want to hurt her, that he was really very concerned that she'd gotten in over her head. I—I made it seem as though Ty had asked my opinion on the best way to untangle himself from an affair he had no more interest in."

"Jess." Ada stopped the movement of her nervous daughter's hands with her own. "Why did you do such a thing?"

"Ty wasn't happy. I'd talked to him just the night before, and he was so down, so unsure of himself. I'd never seen Ty unsure of himself." Her fingers began to move restlessly under her mother's. "It seemed so clear to me that Asher was wrong for him, hurting him. I was convinced I had to save him from being hurt more."

Leaning back, Ada let her gaze drift. The West Side Tennis Club was respectfully dingy, very American. Perhaps that was why she'd always liked it. It was noisy. The Long Island Rail Road ran alongside, competing with helicopters, planes and road traffic. Ada had never completely gotten used to the relative quiet of suburbia after a lifetime in the inner city. Now she sat back, absorbing the noise, trying to think of the right words. It occurred to her that parenting didn't stop when children became adults. Perhaps it never stopped at all.

"Ty loved Asher, Jess."

"I know." Jess stared down at the shredded paper napkin. "I didn't think he did. I thought if he'd loved her, he would have been happy. And if she had loved him, she would have . . . well, she would have acted like all the other women who hung around him."

"Do you think Ty would have loved her if she had been like all the other women?"

Jess flushed, amazing herself and amusing her mother. It was a bit disconcerting to think of the tiny, white-haired Ada Starbuck, mother, grandmother, knowing about passion. "It wasn't until after I met Mac that I realized love doesn't always make you smile and glow," Jess went on, keeping her eyes lowered. "There were times when I was miserable and confused over my feelings for Mac and I began to remember that last talk I had with Ty before I went to see Asher. I realized how alike Ty and I are, how the stronger our feelings are, the more moody we can become."

On a deep breath she met her mother's gaze levelly. "I tried to rationalize that Asher wouldn't have left Ty, that she wouldn't have married Eric if she had really cared. And that if he had, Ty wouldn't have let her go."

"Pride can be just as strong as love. The things you said to Asher made her feel unwanted, and betrayed, I imagine, that Ty would have spoken to you about it."

"If the situation had been reversed, I would have scratched her eyes out and told her to go to hell."

Ada's laugh was a warm, young sound. "Yes, you would. Then you'd have gone to the man you loved and used your claws on him. Asher's different."

"Yes." Miserable, Jess pushed her untouched coffee aside. "Ty always said so. Mom, when they got back together, I was so guilty and frightened. Then I was relieved. And now, I can tell something's gone wrong again." As she had as a child, Jess gave her mother a long, pleading look. "What should I do?"

Strange, Ada mused, that her children wanted to pamper her on one hand, thrusting dishwashers and fancy jewelry on her, while on the other, they still looked to her for all the answers. "You'll have to talk to both of them," Ada said briskly. "Then you'll have to back off and let the two of them work it out. You might be able to heal what you did three years ago, but you can do nothing about what's between them now."

"If they love each other—"

"You made a decision for them once," Ada pointed out. "Don't make the same mistake again."

She hadn't been able to sleep. She hadn't been able to eat. Only the promise she had made to herself never to quit again forced Asher onto the court. Purposely she remained in the dressing room until the last moment to avoid the fans who wandered the walkways and mingled with players. It would take more effort than she could have summoned to smile and make small talk.

When she came outside the humidity hit her like a fist. Shaking off the weakness, Asher went directly to her chair. She heard the applause, but didn't acknowledge it. She couldn't afford to. Even before she began, Asher knew her biggest problem would be concentration.

Her arms ached, her whole body ached and she felt bone-deep exhausted. Pain was something she could ignore once the match was under way, but she wasn't sure she could ignore the jellied weakness inside her, the feeling that someone had punched a yawning hole in the center of her life. Still wearing her warm-up jacket, she took a few experimental swings.

"Asher." Cursing the interruption, she glanced over at Chuck. Concern touched his eyes as he stepped toward her. "Hey, you don't look good. Are you sick?"

"I'm fine."

He studied the shadowed eyes and pale cheeks. "Like hell."

"If I come out on the court, I'm well enough to play," she returned, exchanging one racket for another. "I've got to warm up."

Baffled, Chuck watched her stalk onto the court. It took only a moment of study to see that she wasn't in top form. Chuck moved away to find Ty.

He was in the showers, his eyes closed under the spray. He'd been curt and brief with the press and even briefer with his colleagues. He wasn't in the mood for congratulations. Anger lay curled inside him, undiminished by the physical demands he had placed on himself. He needed more—a sparring match, a marathon run—anything to pump the poison out of his system. Though he heard Chuck call him, Ty remained silent and kept his eyes shut.

"Ty, will you listen to me? Something's wrong with Asher."

Taking his time, Ty stepped back so that the water beat on his chest. Slowly he opened his eyes. "So?"

"So?" Astonished, Chuck gaped at him. "I said something's wrong with Asher."

"I heard you."

"She looks sick," Chuck continued, certain that Ty didn't comprehend. "I just saw her. She shouldn't be playing today. She looks awful."

Ty fought the instinctive need to go to her. He could remember vividly the scene the night before. With a flick of the wrist he shut off the shower. "Asher knows what she's doing. She makes her own decisions."

Too stunned to be angry, Chuck stared at him. He'd never seen Ty look cold any more than he'd ever seen Asher look furious. Until today. "What the devil's going on here?" he demanded. "I just told you your woman's sick."

Ty felt the tightening in his belly and ignored it. "She's not my woman." Grabbing a towel, he secured it lightly around his waist.

After dragging a hand through his hair, Chuck followed Ty into the locker room. He'd known since that morning when he and Ty had practiced together that something was wrong. Accustomed to his friend's mercurial moods, he had dismissed it, assuming Ty and Asher had had a lover's quarrel. But no lover's quarrel would make Ty indifferent to Asher's health.

"Look, if you two have had a fight, that's no reason—"

"I said she's not my woman." Ty's voice was deadly calm as he pulled on jeans.

"Fine," Chuck snapped. "Then if the field's clear, I might just try my luck." He was slammed back against the lockers, feet dangling as Ty grabbed his shirt in both hands, jerking him up. Coolly, Chuck looked into the stormy eyes. "Not your woman, friend?" he said softly. "Tell that to somebody who doesn't know you."

Breathing hard, Ty struggled against the need to strike back. The hours of violent tennis hadn't drained the anger or the grief. Without a word he dropped Chuck to his feet, then snatched a shirt from his locker.

"Are you going out there?" Chuck demanded. "Somebody should stop her before she makes whatever's wrong with her worse. You know damn well she isn't going to listen to me."

"Don't push me." Ty dragged the shirt over his head before he slammed the locker door. This time Chuck kept his silence. He heard the tremor in Ty's voice and recognized that the emotion wasn't anger. Only once before had he seen his friend this torn apart. It had been Asher then, as it was obviously Asher now. With warring loyalties, he reached out.

"Okay, you want to talk about it?"

"No." Clenching his fists, Ty fought to regain his control. "No, just go on out . . . keep an eye on her."

She was fighting, and losing. Asher had used almost all her reserves of energy to take the first set to a tie breaker. The ultimate loss had taken its emotional toll. Kingston was a crafty enough player to sense her opponent's flagging stamina and capitalized on it. Precision was nothing without strength. Asher's strength was ebbing quickly.

The noise played havoc with her concentration. Already playing below par, she needed the sound of the ball hitting the racket. Engines drowned it out, denying her the sense of hearing. On the brittle grass the ball jumped, skidded and stopped. Top speed was necessary, and she didn't have it.

Unable to prevent himself, Ty came to the edge of the tunnel to watch. Immediately he could see that Chuck hadn't exaggerated. She was too pale, too slow. Instinctively he took a step forward. Restraining himself was more difficult than going on, but he stopped, cursing her even as he cursed himself. She'd made her own choice. She herself had cut off any right he had to influence her. From where he stood he could hear her labored breathing, see the strain she fought to keep from her face. At the twinge of fresh pain he turned away from the court.

With a blind determination that was more nerves than power, Asher had taken the second set to three–all. Her face shone with sweat. Weakened, Asher knew that she would have to find a hole in

Kingston's game soon, and have the wit and stamina to exploit it. Grit was a weapon, but not weapon enough against power, precision and cunning.

At double break point Asher prepared to serve again. If she could pull this one out, she'd have a chance. If Kingston broke her serve, the match was as good as over. *Concentrate, concentrate,* she ordered herself as she gave the ball a few testing bounces. She counted each one, trying to calm herself. Ty's furious, accusing words hammered in her brain. His face, enraged and stricken, floated in front of her eyes. Tossing the ball, Asher drove at it with her racket.

"Fault."

She shut her eyes and cursed. Control, she ordered herself. If she lost control now, she lost everything. As she took an extra moment, the crowd began to hum in speculation.

"Come on, Face, let's see what you're made of!"

Gritting her teeth, Asher put everything she had left into the serve. The ace brought a roar of approval. She wasn't beaten yet.

But her next serve was soft. Slapping it back to her, Kingston incited a hard, punishing rally. Asher battled by instinct, all reserve depleted. Her eyes, her mind, were fixed on the ball and the ball only. Dodging after a slice, she skidded, barely meeting it with her racket as she stumbled. She went down to her knees, crumbling into a ball of exhaustion and pain.

Someone's hands hooked under her armpits, pulling her to her feet. Asher pushed them away blindly to stagger to her chair.

"Come on, Asher." Chuck toweled off her streaming face, talking to her as she drew in ragged, straining breaths. "Come on, babe, you're not in any shape to be out here today. I'll help you inside."

"No." She shook off his hand. "No, I won't forfeit." Rising, she dropped the towel to the ground. "I'm going to finish."

Helpless, Chuck watched her fight a losing battle.

Asher slept for almost twenty-four hours straight. Her body recharged as she lay motionless in the bed she had shared so recently with Ty. The loss of the match—and the Grand Slam—meant little. She'd finished. Her pride was whole because she had refused to give up, because she had managed to face the reporters after the match and give them a calm accounting. When they had speculated on the state of her health, she'd told them she'd been fit to play. She would give no excuses for losing. If there was blame, it lay within herself. That was the primary rule of the game.

On returning to her room, Asher only took time to strip to her underwear before falling exhausted onto the bed. Sleep came immediately. Hours later she didn't hear the door open or Ty's footsteps as he crossed to the bedroom to look at her.

Asher lay flat on her stomach across the spread—something he knew she did only when absolutely depleted. Her breathing was deep, a heavy sound of fatigue. The hands he had thrust in his pockets balled into fists.

His emotions were pulling in too many directions. She shouldn't be allowed to do this to him, he thought furiously. She shouldn't make him want to hurt and protect at the same time. Walking to the window, he remained silent for a quarter of an hour, listening to her breathe. Before he left her, Ty drew the drapes closed so that the sunlight wouldn't disturb her.

When Asher awoke, a full day had passed. The aches made themselves known.

Keeping her mind a blank, she ran a hot tub. As the water lapped over her, she slipped into a half doze. Asher heard the knock on the door, and ignored it. The phone rang, but she didn't open her eyes.

Disturbed, Jess replaced the receiver after ten full rings. Where could Asher be? she wondered. She knew Asher was still registered at the hotel, but she hadn't answered the phone or the door in more than a day. She'd tried to tell Ty, but he simply wouldn't listen. Any more than he'd listened to her attempts at confession.

Her conscience plagued her. She hadn't tried hard enough, Jess berated herself. She'd been so afraid of losing Ty's love, she had allowed him to brush her off when she tried to talk to him. Well, no more, she determined.

Checking her watch, Jess calculated that Ty would be preparing for the day's match. She cursed, then fretted, then made herself a promise. When it was over, win or lose, she was going to corner her brother and make him listen until she'd told him everything.

Now that the vow had been made, Jess discovered that the waiting wasn't easy. In the stands she marked time. Ty played with the same fierce anger she had observed in his quarter-final match. It was just as effective.

Beneath her pride in him was the constant thought that her brother might turn away from her after he'd heard her out. But Jess sat patiently through the match and through the press conference. She'd left it to her mother to persuade Martin to go back to the hotel instead of dragging Ty off for a replay of the match. Like a tennis groupie, Jess waited for Ty to emerge from the locker room, then pounced.

"Ty, I need to talk to you."

"I'm talked out, Jess." He patted her hand, then removed it from his arm. "I want to get out of here before the next sportswriter latches onto me."

"Fine, I'll drive. You'll listen."

"Look, Jess—"

"Now, Ty."

Annoyed, Ty stalked to the car. For the first time in his life he wished his family hadn't come. He'd managed to avoid them for the most part, using fatigue or practice as excuses. His mother knew him too well, and her silence questioned him constantly. Martin was ecstatic, wanting to analyze every volley and shower praise. And the hardest of all was watching Pete, darting here and there, babbling, laughing, reminding Ty of something that might have been.

"Look, Jess, I'm tired—"

"Just get in," she interrupted tersely. "I've already put this off for too long."

They slammed their doors simultaneously. Not a very auspicious start, she mused as she merged with traffic, but she'd never finish if she didn't begin. "Okay, I've got some things to tell you, and I'd like you to hear me out before you say anything."

"Unless I want to hitch a damn ride back, I don't have much choice, do I?"

She sent him a worried look. "Don't hate me, Ty."

"Oh, come on, Jess." Ashamed of wishing her away, he gave her hair a quick tousle. "I might be mad at being shanghaied, but I'm not going to hate you."

"Just listen," she started. Staring straight ahead, she began.

At first, Ty paid little attention. She was hopping back to the summer he had first been with Asher. He started once to interrupt, not wanting to be reminded. Jess shook her head fiercely and silenced him. With strained patience Ty sat back and watched the passing scenery.

When Jess told him that she had gone to see Asher, his brows lowered. His concentration focused. Listening to her pouring out the things she had said—*Ty's tired of you. . . . He doesn't know exactly how to end things without hurting you*—his rage built swiftly. Jess felt the fury swirling, and barely paused for breath.

"She seemed to have no reaction to anything I said. She was very cool, totally in control of herself. It just seemed to reinforce what I thought of her." Stopping for a light, Jess swallowed quickly. "I didn't understand how anyone could have strong feelings and not express them, not then. After I met Mac I realized . . ." When the light changed she gunned the motor with a jerk of her foot, then stalled the engine. On a frustrated oath she started the car again as Ty remained silent.

"When I looked back on it," Jess continued after a shaky breath, "I remember how pale she got, how quiet. It wasn't indifference, but shock. She listened to everything I said, never raising her voice or shedding a tear. I must have hurt her terribly."

Her voice broke and she waited for him to speak, but there was nothing but thick, vibrant silence. "I had no right, Ty," Jess continued quickly. "I know that. I wanted—I wanted to help, to pay you back somehow for everything you'd done for me. At the time, I thought I was telling her the things you couldn't bring yourself to. I'd convinced myself . . . Oh, I don't know." Jess made a quick gesture with her hand before she gripped the gear shift. "Maybe I was even jealous, but I didn't think you loved her and I was so sure she didn't love you. Especially when she married so quickly."

Because tears were forming, she pulled over to the side of the road. "Ty, to tell you I'm sorry isn't enough, but I don't have anything else."

The silence in the car vibrated for the space of three heartbeats. "What made you think you could play God with my life?" Ty demanded in a sudden burst that had her jolting. "Who the hell put you in charge?"

Forcing herself to meet his eyes, Jess spoke quietly. "There's nothing you can say to me I haven't said to myself, but you're entitled."

"Do you have any idea what you did to my life?"

She shuddered involuntarily. "Yes."

"I was going to ask Asher to marry me that night, the night I got back and found you in our room. The night you told me she'd gone off with Wickerton."

"Oh, God, Ty." Choking back a sob, Jess laid her head on the steering wheel. "I never thought . . . I never realized she meant that much to you."

"She was everything I wanted, don't you understand? Everything! I was half crazy because I wasn't sure she'd say yes." He drummed his fist against the dash. "And, God, I'm still not sure. I'll never be sure." The anguish in his voice made Jess straighten.

"Ty, if you'd go see her. If you'd—"

"No." He thought again of the child. His child. "There are other reasons now."

"I'll go," Jess began. "I can—"

"No!" The word whipped out at her, causing Jess to swallow the rest of the sentence. "Stay away from her."

"All right," she agreed unsteadily. "If that's the way you want it."

"That's the way I want it."

"You still love her," Jess asked.

Ty turned his head so that his eyes met his sister's. "Yes, I love her. That isn't always enough, Jess. I don't think I'd ever be able to forget . . ."

"Forget?" she prompted when he trailed off. "Forget what?"

"Something she took from me . . ." Angry energy built up again, grinding at his nerves. "I've got to walk."

"Ty." Jess stopped him with a tentative hand on the arm as he jerked open the door of the car. "Do you want me to go away—back to California? I can make up an excuse, even leave Pete and Mac here for the rest of the tournament. I won't stay for the finals if it upsets you."

"Do what you want," he told her shortly. He started to slam the door of the car when he caught the look in her eyes. He'd protected her all of his life, too long to change now. Love was rooted in him. "It's history, Jess," he said in calmer tones. "Past history. Forget it."

Turning, Ty walked away, hoping he'd be able to believe his own words.

Chapter Twelve

 $\mathcal{A}$sher sat on the bed to watch the men's singles championship. The television commentary barely penetrated as she judged and dissected each stroke and volley for herself. She couldn't go to the stadium, but nothing would prevent her from watching Ty compete.

On the close-ups, she studied his face carefully. Yes, some strain showed, she noted, but his concentration was complete. His energy was as volatile as ever, perhaps more so. For that she could be grateful.

Each time they replayed a shot in slow motion, Asher could fully appreciate the beauty of his form. Muscles rippled as he stretched; feet left the turf in a leap for more power. He was a raw athlete with anger simmering just under the discipline. The graphite racket was no more than an extension of the arm that was whipping the ball harder and faster. As always, his hair flew around the sweatband, dramatic and unruly. His eyes were dark with a rage barely contained. Was it the game that drove him? she wondered. The insatiable thirst to win? Or were there other emotions pushing him this time?

If there were, it was easy to see that they added to the impetus. He was an explosion heating up, a storm rumbling just overhead. Asher knew him well enough to recognize that his control balanced on a very thin edge, but it made his game all the more exciting.

His topspin drove to Chuck's backhand and was returned, power for power. A slice, a lob, an overhead. Turned the wrong way, Chuck pivoted, sprinted, but had no chance to return. The call was late, judging Ty's ball long.

His head whipped around to the judge, his eyes deadly. Asher shuddered when the camera zoomed in so that the undisguised fury seemed aimed directly at her. For a moment they seemed to stare into each other's eyes. Disgust warred with temper before he turned to resume his receiving stance. Crouched like a cat, his eyes intense, he waited. Asher let out an unsteady breath.

Ty was judging the bounce with uncanny accuracy. If it threatened to die, he was under it. When it chose to soar, he got behind it. With unrelenting challenge he charged the net. He baited Chuck, dared him, and, time after time, outwitted him. His game was all aggression and power—Starbuck at his best, she thought with undiminished pride. He could demoralize even a seasoned pro like Chuck with a lightning-fast return that lifted chalk from the service line. With each swing she could hear the grunt of exertion and the swish of air. How she wanted to be there.

He wouldn't want her. She wouldn't soon forget that look of rage and disgust he had turned on her—too much like the one his video image had projected. A man like Starbuck had no ambivalent emotions. It was love or hate; she'd felt them both.

She'd been cut out of his life. She had to accept that. She had to . . . quit? Asher asked herself. Suddenly her chin rose. Was that what she was doing again? She looked back at the screen as the camera zoomed in on Ty's face. His eyes were opaque and dangerous before he went into a full stretch for his serve. The force of her feelings attacked her. She loved and wanted and needed.

No, damn it! Rising, Asher cursed him. No, if she was going to lose, she was going down fighting, just as she had on the courts. He wouldn't brush her out of his life so easily this time. Briefly she'd forgotten that she no longer aimed her actions at pleasing those around her. Perhaps he didn't want to see her, but that was just too bad. He would see her . . . and he would listen.

Just as she snapped off the set, a knock sounded on her door. Battling impatience, Asher went to answer. Her expression changed from grim determination to wonder.

"Dad!"

"Asher." Jim met her stunned exclamation with an unsmiling nod. "May I come in?"

He hadn't changed, she thought wildly. He hadn't

changed at all. He was still tall and tanned and silvery-blond. He was still her father. Her eyes filled with love and tears. "Oh, Dad, I'm so glad to see you." Grasping his hand, she drew him into the room. Then the awkwardness set in. "Sit down, please." While gesturing to a chair, Asher sought something to fill the gap. "Shall I order up something to drink? Some coffee?"

"No." He sat as she suggested and looked at his daughter. She was thinner, he noted. And nervous, as nervous as he was himself. Since Ty's phone call, he'd done little but think of her. "Asher," he began, then sighed. "Please sit down." He waited until she settled across from him. "I want to tell you I'm proud of the way you've played this season."

His voice was stiff, but she expected little else. "Thank you."

"I'm most proud of the last match you played."

Asher gave him a small smile. How typical that it was tennis he spoke of first. "I lost."

"You played," he countered. "Right down to the last point, you played. I wonder how many people who watched knew that you were ill."

"I wasn't ill," Asher corrected him automatically. "If I came on court—"

"Then you were fit," he finished, before he shook his head. "I drummed that into you well, didn't I?"

"A matter of pride and sportmanship," she said quietly, giving him back the words he had given her again and again during her training.

Jim lapsed into silence, frowning at the elegant hands that lay folded in her lap. She'd always been his princess, he thought, his beautiful, golden princess. He'd wanted to give her the world, and he'd wanted her to deserve it.

"I didn't intend to come here to see you."

If the statement hurt, she gave no sign. "What changed your mind?"

"A couple of things, most particularly, your last match."

Rising, Asher walked to the window. "So, I had to lose to have you speak to me again." The words came easily, as did the light trace of bitterness. Though love had remained constant, she found no need to give him unvarnished adulation any longer. "All those years I needed you so badly, I waited, hoping you'd forgive me."

"It was a hard thing to forgive, Asher."

He rose, too, realizing his daughter had grown stronger. He wasn't sure how to approach the woman she had become.

"It was a hard thing to accept," she countered in the calm voice he remembered. "That my father looked at me as athlete first and child second."

"That's not true."

"Isn't it?" Turning, she fixed him with a level stare. "You turned your back on me because I gave up my career. Not once when I was suffering did you hold out a hand to me. I had no one to go to but you, and because you said no, I had no one at all."

"I tried to deal with it. I tried to accept your decision to marry that man, though you knew how I felt about him." The unexpected guilt angered him and chilled his voice. "I tried to understand how you could give up what you were to play at being something else."

"I had no choice," she began furiously.

"No choice?" His derision was sharp as a blade. "You made your own decision, Asher—your career for a title—just as you made it about the child. My grandchild."

"Please." She lifted both hands to her temples as she turned away. "Please don't. Have you any idea how much and how often I've paid for that moment of carelessness?"

"Carelessness?" Stunned into disbelief, Jim stared at the back of her head. "You call the conception of a child carelessness?"

"No, *no!*" Her voice trembled as it rose. "The loss. If I hadn't let myself get upset, if I had looked where I was going, I never would have fallen. I never would have lost Ty's child."

"What!" As the pain slammed into his stomach, Jim sank into the chair. "Fallen? Ty's child? *Ty's?*" He ran a hand over his eyes as he tried to sort it out. Suddenly he felt old and frail and frightened. "Asher, are you telling me you miscarried Ty's child?"

"Yes." Wearily she turned back to face him. "I wrote you, I told you."

"If you wrote, I never received the letter." Shaken, Jim held out a hand, waiting until she grasped it. "Asher, Eric told me you aborted his child." For an instant, the words, their meaning, failed to penetrate. Her look was blank and vulnerable enough to make him feel every year of his age. "A calculated abortion of your husband's child," he said deliberately. When she swayed he gripped her other hand. "He told me you'd done so without his knowledge or permission. He seemed devastated. I believed him, Asher." As she went limp, he drew her down to her knees in front of him. "I believed him."

"Oh, God." Her eyes were huge and dark with shock.

Her father's fingers trembled in hers. "He phoned me from London. He sounded half mad—I thought with grief. He said that you hadn't told him until after it was done. That you had told him you wanted no children to interfere with the life you intended to build as Lady Wickerton."

Too numb for anger, Asher shook her head. "I didn't know even Eric could be so vindictive, so cruel."

It all began to make horrid sense. Her letters to her father hadn't been answered. Eric had seen that they were never mailed. Then, when she had phoned him, Jim had been cold and brief. He'd told her that he could never resolve himself to her choice. Asher had assumed he meant her rejection of her career.

"He wanted me to pay," she explained as she dropped her head on her father's lap. "He never wanted me to stop paying."

Gently Jim cupped her face in his hands. "Tell me everything. I'll listen, as I should have a long time ago."

She started with Jess, leaving nothing out including her final stormy estrangement from Ty. Jim's mouth tightened at her recounting of the accident and the hospital scene with Eric. Listening, he cursed himself for being a fool.

"And now, Ty . . ." As realization struck her, she

paled. "Ty thinks—Eric must have told him I'd had an abortion."

"No, I told him."

"You?" Confused, Asher pressed her fingers to the headache in her temple. "But how—"

"He called me a few nights ago. He wanted to convince me to see you. I told him enough to make him believe the lie just as I'd believed it."

"That night when I woke up," Asher remembered. "Oh, my God, when he realized it had been his baby . . . The things he was saying! I couldn't think at the time." She shut her eyes. "No wonder he hates me."

Color flooded back into her face. "I have to tell him the truth and make him believe it." Scrambling up, she dashed for the door. "I'll go to the club. I have to make him listen. I have to make him understand."

"The match must be nearly over." Jim rose on unsteady legs. His daughter had been through hell, and he had done nothing but add to it. "You'll never catch him there."

Frustrated, Asher looked at her watch. "I don't know where he's staying." Releasing the doorknob, she went to the phone. "I'll just have to find out."

"Asher . . ." Awkward, unsure, Jim held out his hand. "Forgive me."

Asher stared into his face as she replaced the receiver. Ignoring the hand, she went into his arms.

It was nearly midnight when Ty reached the door of his room. For the past two hours he'd been drinking steadily. Celebrating. It wasn't every day you won the Grand Slam, he reminded himself as he searched for his keys. And it wasn't every day a man had a half dozen women offering to share their beds with him. He gave a snort of laughter as he slid the key into the lock. And why the hell hadn't he taken one of them up on it?

None of them was Asher. He shook away the thought as he struggled to make the doorknob function. No, he simply hadn't wanted a woman, Ty told himself. It was because he was tired and had had too much to drink. Asher was yesterday.

The hotel room was dark as he stumbled inside. If he was right about nothing else, he was right about having too much to drink. Through glass after glass Ty had told himself the liquor was for celebrating, not for forgetting. The kid from the Chicago slum had made it to the top, in spades.

The hell with it, he decided, tossing his keys into the room. With a thud they landed on the carpet. Swaying a bit, he stripped off his shirt and threw it in the same direction. Now if he could just find his way to the bed without turning on a light, he'd sleep. Tonight he'd sleep—with enough liquor in his system to anesthetize him. There'd be no dreams of soft skin or dark blue eyes tonight.

As he fumbled toward the bedroom, a light switched on, blinding him. With a pungent curse Ty covered his eyes, balancing himself with one hand on the wall.

"Turn that damn thing off," he muttered.

"Well, the victor returns triumphant."

The quiet voice had him lowering the hand from

his eyes. Asher sat primly in a chair, looking unruffled, soft and utterly tempting. Ty felt desire work its way through the alcohol.

"What the hell are you doing here?"

"And very drunk," she said as if he hadn't spoken. Rising, she went to him. "I suppose you deserve it after the way you played today. Should I add my congratulations to the host of others?"

"Get out." He pushed away from the wall. "I don't want you."

"I'll order up some coffee," she said calmly. "We'll talk."

"I said get out!" Catching her wrist, he whirled her around. "Before I lose my temper and hurt you."

Though her pulse jumped under his fingers, she stood firm. "I'll leave after we talk."

"Do you know what I want to do to you?" he demanded, shoving her back against the wall. "Do you know that I want to beat you senseless?"

"Yes." She didn't cringe as his fury raged down on her. "Ty, if you'll listen—"

"I don't want to listen to you." The image of her lying exhausted on the bed raced through his mind. "Get out while I can still stop myself from hurting you."

"I can't." She lifted a hand to his cheek. "Ty—"

Her words were cut off as he pressed her back into the wall. For an instant she thought he would strike her, then his mouth came down on hers, bruising, savage. He forced her lips apart, thrusting his tongue deep as she struggled. His teeth ground against hers as though to punish them both. There was the faint taste of liquor, reminding her he had drink as well as anger in his system. When she tried to turn her head, he caught her face in his hand—not gently, in the touch she remembered, but viselike.

He could smell her—the soft talc, the lightly sexy perfume. And the fear. She made a small, pleading sound before she stopped fighting him. Without being aware of what he did, he lightened the grip to a caress. His lips gentled on hers, tasting, savoring. Mumbling her name, he trailed kisses over her skin until he felt the essence of her flowing back into him. God, how he'd missed her.

"I can't do without you," he whispered. "I can't." He sank to the floor, drawing her down with him.

He was lost in her—the feel, the taste, the fragrance. His mind was too full of Asher to allow him to think. Sensation ruled him, trembling along his skin to follow the path of her fingers. It was as if she sought to soothe and arouse him at once. He was helpless to resist her—or his need for her. As if in a trance, he took his lips over her, missing nothing as his hunger seemed insatiable. Her quickening breaths were like music, setting his rhythm.

The air grew steamier as his hands homed in on secrets that made her moan. Her body shuddered into life. No longer gentle, but demanding, she tangled her fingers in his hair and guided him to sweet spaces he'd neglected. Then ever greedy, ever giving, she drew him back to her mouth. Her tongue toyed with his lips, then slid inside to drink up all the flavors. His head swimming, he answered the kiss.

The need for her was unreasonable, but Ty was beyond reason. Without her there'd been an emptiness that even his fury couldn't fill. Now the void was closing. She was in his blood, in his bone, so essential a part of him he had been able to find no place of separation. Now there was no will to do so.

Under him, she was moving, inviting, entreating. He whispered a denial against her mouth, but his pounding blood took control. He was inside her without being aware of it. Then all sensation spiraled together in an intensity that made him cry out. And it was her name he spoke, in both ecstasy and in despair.

Drained, Ty rolled from her to stare at the ceiling. How could he have let that happen? he demanded. How could he have felt such love, found such pleasure in a woman he had vowed to amputate from his life? He wondered now if he'd ever find the strength to stay away from her. Life with her, and life without her, would be two kinds of hell.

"Ty." Reaching over, Asher touched his shoulder.

"Don't." Without looking at her he rose. "Get dressed, for God's sake," he muttered as he tugged on his own jeans with trembling hands. Who had used whom? he wondered. "Do you have a car?"

Sitting up, Asher pushed her hair out of her face. Hair, she remembered, that only moments before he had been kissing. "No."

"I'll call you a cab."

"That won't be necessary." In silence she began to dress. "I realize you're sorry that this happened."

"I'm damned if I'll apologize," he snapped.

"I wasn't asking you to," she told him quietly. "I was going to say that I'm not sorry. I love you, and

making love with you is only one way to show it."
She managed, after three attempts, to button her
blouse. When she looked up, he was at the window,
his back to her. "Ty, I came here to tell you some
things you must know. When I'm finished, I'll go and
give you time to think about them."

"Can't you understand I don't want to think
anymore?"

"It's the last thing I'll ask of you."

"All right." In a gesture of fatigue she rarely saw
in him, he rubbed both hands over his face. The
liquor had burned out of his system—by the anger or
the passion, he wasn't sure. But he was cold sober.
"Maybe I should tell you first that what Jess said to
you three years ago was her own fabrication. I didn't
know anything about it until the other day when she
told me what she'd done. In her own way, she was
trying to protect me."

"I don't understand what you're talking about."

Turning, he gave her a grim smile. "Did you really
think I was tired of you? Looking for a way out?
Wondering how I could ditch you without raising too
much fuss or interfering with my career?"

Asher opened her mouth to speak, then shut it
again. How strange that the words still hurt and
made her defensive.

"Obviously you did."

"And if I did?" she countered. "Everything she
said fit. You'd never made a commitment to me.
There'd never been any talk about the future."

"On either side," he reminded her.

Asher pushed away the logic. "If you'd once told
me—"

"Or perhaps you were uncertain enough of your own feelings that when Jess dumped that on you, you ran right to Wickerton. Even though you were carrying my baby."

"I didn't know I was pregnant when I married Eric." She saw him shrug her words away. In fury she grabbed both of his arms. "I tell you I didn't know! Perhaps if I had known before I would have simply gone away. I don't know what I would have done. I was already terrified you were growing tired of me before Jess confirmed it."

"And where the hell did you get a stupid idea like that?"

"You'd been so moody, so withdrawn. Everything she said made sense."

"If I was moody and withdrawn, it was because I was trying to work out the best way to ask Asher Wolfe, Miss Society Tennis, to marry Starbuck, from the wrong side of the tracks."

Asher took an uncertain step toward him. "You would have married me?"

"I still have the ring I bought you," he answered.

"A ring?" she repeated stupidly. "You'd bought me a ring?" For some inexplicable reason the thought of it stunned her more than anything else.

"I'd planned to try a very conventional proposal. And if that didn't work, maybe a kidnapping."

She tried to laugh because tears were entirely too close. "It would have worked."

"If you'd told me you were pregnant—"

"Ty, I didn't know! Damn it!" She pounded once against his chest. "Do you think I would have married Eric if I had known? It was weeks afterward that I found out."

"Why the hell didn't you tell me then?"

"Do you think I wanted to get you back that way?" The old pride lifted her chin. "And I was married to another man. I'd made him a promise."

"A promise that meant more than the life of the child we'd made together," he retorted bitterly. "A promise that let you walk into one of those antiseptic clinics and destroy something innocent and beautiful. And mine."

The image was too ugly, the truth too painful. Flying at him, Asher struck him again and again until he pinned her hands behind her back. *"And mine!"* she shouted at him. "And mine, or doesn't my part matter?"

"You didn't want it." His fingers closed like steel as she tried to pull away. "But you didn't have the decency to ask me if I did. Couldn't you bear the thought of carrying part of me inside you for nine months?"

"Don't ask me what I could bear." She wasn't pale now, but vivid with fury. "I didn't have an abortion," she spat at him. "I miscarried. I miscarried and nearly died in the process. Would you feel better if I had? God knows I tried to."

"Miscarried?" His grip shifted from her wrists to her shoulders. "What are you talking about?"

"Eric hated me too!" she shouted. "When I learned I was pregnant and told him, all he could say was that I'd deceived him. I'd tried to trick him into claiming the baby after you'd refused me. Nothing I said got through to him. We argued and argued. We were near the steps and he was shouting. All I wanted to do was get away." Her hands flew up to cover her face as she remembered again, all too clearly. "I didn't look, I only ran. Then I was falling. I tried to stop, but my head hit the railing, I think. Then I don't remember anything until I woke up and the baby was gone."

Somehow he could see it as vividly as though it were being played on film in front of his eyes. "Oh, God, Asher." When he tried to take her in his arms, she pulled away.

"I wanted you, but I knew you'd never forgive me. It didn't seem to matter anymore, so I did what Eric wanted." To force back the tears, she pressed her fingers to her eyes. "I didn't want you to know, I couldn't have stood it if you had known when you didn't want me." Lowering her hands, she looked at him, dry-eyed. "I paid for losing your baby, Ty. For three years I did without everything that mattered to me, and I grieved alone. I can't mourn any longer."

"No." Going to the window, he flung it up as if he needed air. There was no breeze, nothing to relieve the burning that he felt. "You've had years to deal with it. I've had days." And she'd had no one, he thought. Years with no one. Ty took several long breaths. "How badly were you hurt?"

Puzzled by the question, she shook her head. "What?"

"Were you badly hurt?" The question was rough and turbulent. When she remained silent he turned. "When you fell, how bad was it?"

"I—I lost the baby."

"I asked about you."

She stared without comprehension. No one had asked her that, not even her father. Looking into Ty's ravaged face, she could only shake her head again.

"Damn it, Asher, did you have a concussion, did you break any bones? You said you almost died."

"The baby died," she repeated numbly.

Crossing to her, he grabbed her shoulders. *"You!"* he shouted. "Don't you know that you're the most important thing to me? We can have a dozen babies if you want. I need to know what happened to you."

"I don't remember very much. I was sedated. There were transfusions . . ." The full impact of his words penetrated slowly. The anguish in his eyes was for her. "Ty." Burying her face against his chest, she clung. "All that's over."

"I should have been with you." He drew her closer. "We should have gone through that together."

"Just tell me you love me. Say the words."

"You know that I do." He cupped her chin to force her head back. "I love you." He saw the first tear fall and kissed it away. "Don't," he pleaded. "No more tears, Face. No more grieving."

She held him close again until the fullness left her chest. "No more grieving," she repeated, and lifted her face.

He touched it gently, fingertips only. "I hurt you."

"We let other people hurt us," she contradicted. "Never again."

"How could we be stupid enough to almost lose it

all twice?" he wondered aloud. "No more secrets, Asher."

She shook her head. "No more secrets. A third chance, Ty?"

"I work best under pressure." He brushed his lips over her temple. "Double break point, Face, I'm on a winning streak."

"You should be celebrating."

"I did my share."

"Not with me." She gave him a light kiss full of promise. "We could go to my place. Pick up a bottle of champagne on the way."

"We could stay here," he countered. "And worry about the champagne tomorrow."

"It is tomorrow," she reminded him.

"Then we've got all day." He began to pull her toward the bedroom.

"Wait a minute." Snatching her hand away, she stepped back. "I'd like to hear that conventional proposal now."

"Come on, Asher." He made another grab for her hand, but she eluded him.

"I mean it."

Flustered, he stuck his hands into his pockets. "You know I want you to marry me."

"That's not a conventional proposal." She folded her arms and waited. "Well," she began when he remained silent, "should I write you a cheat sheet? You say something like, Asher—"

"I know what I'm supposed to say," he muttered. "I'd rather try the kidnapping."

Laughing, she walked over and twined her arms

around his neck. "Ask me," she whispered, letting her lips hover an inch from his.

"Will you marry me, Asher?" The lips held tantalizingly near his curved, but she remained silent. His eyes dropped to them, lingered, then rose to hers. "Well?"

"I'm thinking it over," she told him. "I was hoping for something a bit more flowery, maybe some poetry or—" The wind was knocked out of her as he hefted her over his shoulder. "Yes, that's good too," she decided. "I should be able to let you know in a few days."

From the height he dropped her, she bounced twice before she settled on the bed.

"Or sooner," she decided as he began unbuttoning her blouse.

"Shut up."

She cocked a brow. "Don't you want to hear my answer?"

"We'll get the license tomorrow."

"I haven't said—"

"And the blood tests."

"I haven't agreed—"

His mouth silenced her in a long, lingering kiss as his body fit unerringly to hers.

"Of course," Asher sighed, "I could probably be persuaded."

MORE ROMANCE FOR
A SPECIAL WAY TO RELAX

$2.25 each

79 ☐ Hastings	105 ☐ Sinclair	131 ☐ Lee	157 ☐ Taylor
80 ☐ Douglass	106 ☐ John	132 ☐ Dailey	158 ☐ Charles
81 ☐ Thornton	107 ☐ Ross	133 ☐ Douglass	159 ☐ Camp
82 ☐ McKenna	108 ☐ Stephens	134 ☐ Ripy	160 ☐ Wisdom
83 ☐ Major	109 ☐ Beckman	135 ☐ Seger	161 ☐ Stanford
84 ☐ Stephens	110 ☐ Browning	136 ☐ Scott	162 ☐ Roberts
85 ☐ Beckman	111 ☐ Thorne	137 ☐ Parker	163 ☐ Halston
86 ☐ Halston	112 ☐ Belmont	138 ☐ Thornton	164 ☐ Ripy
87 ☐ Dixon	113 ☐ Camp	139 ☐ Halston	165 ☐ Lee
88 ☐ Saxon	114 ☐ Ripy	140 ☐ Sinclair	166 ☐ John
89 ☐ Meriwether	115 ☐ Halston	141 ☐ Saxon	167 ☐ Hurley
90 ☐ Justin	116 ☐ Roberts	142 ☐ Bergen	168 ☐ Thornton
91 ☐ Stanford	117 ☐ Converse	143 ☐ Bright	169 ☐ Beckman
92 ☐ Hamilton	118 ☐ Jackson	144 ☐ Meriwether	170 ☐ Paige
93 ☐ Lacey	119 ☐ Langan	145 ☐ Wallace	171 ☐ Gray
94 ☐ Barrie	120 ☐ Dixon	146 ☐ Thornton	172 ☐ Hamilton
95 ☐ Doyle	121 ☐ Shaw	147 ☐ Dalton	173 ☐ Belmont
96 ☐ Baxter	122 ☐ Walker	148 ☐ Gordon	174 ☐ Dixon
97 ☐ Shaw	123 ☐ Douglass	149 ☐ Claire	175 ☐ Roberts
98 ☐ Hurley	124 ☐ Mikels	150 ☐ Dailey	176 ☐ Walker
99 ☐ Dixon	125 ☐ Cates	151 ☐ Shaw	177 ☐ Howard
100 ☐ Roberts	126 ☐ Wildman	152 ☐ Adams	178 ☐ Bishop
101 ☐ Bergen	127 ☐ Taylor	153 ☐ Sinclair	179 ☐ Meriwether
102 ☐ Wallace	128 ☐ Macomber	154 ☐ Malek	180 ☐ Jackson
103 ☐ Taylor	129 ☐ Rowe	155 ☐ Lacey	181 ☐ Browning
104 ☐ Wallace	130 ☐ Carr	156 ☐ Hastings	182 ☐ Thornton

Silhouette Special Edition

$2.25 each

183 ☐ Sinclair	189 ☐ Ripy	195 ☐ Griffin	201 ☐ Dalton
184 ☐ Daniels	190 ☐ Wisdom	196 ☐ Cates	202 ☐ Thornton
185 ☐ Gordon	191 ☐ Hardy	197 ☐ Lind	203 ☐ Parker
186 ☐ Scott	192 ☐ Taylor	198 ☐ Bishop	204 ☐ Eagle
187 ☐ Stanford	193 ☐ John	199 ☐ Roberts	
188 ☐ Lacey	194 ☐ Jackson	200 ☐ Milan	

SILHOUETTE SPECIAL EDITION, Department SE/2
1230 Avenue of the Americas
New York, NY 10020

Please send me the books I have checked above. I am enclosing $_____
(please add 75¢ to cover postage and handling. NYS and NYC residents please
add appropriate sales tax). Send check or money order—no cash or C.O.D.'s
please. Allow six weeks for delivery.

NAME _____

ADDRESS _____

CITY _____ STATE/ZIP _____

Silhouette Special Edition

Fall in love again for the first time every time you read a Silhouette Romance novel.

Take 4 books free—no strings attached.

Step into the world of Silhouette Romance, and experience love as thrilling as you always knew it could be. In each enchanting 192-page novel, you'll travel with lighthearted young heroines to lush, exotic lands where love and tender romance wait to carry you away.

Get 6 books each month before they are available anywhere else! Act now and we'll send you four touching Silhouette Romance novels. They're our gift to introduce you to our convenient home subscription service. Every month, we'll send you six new Silhouette Romance books. Look them over for 15 days. If you keep them, pay just $11.70 for all six. Or return them at no charge.

We'll mail your books to you *two full months before they are available anywhere else*. Plus, with every shipment, you'll receive the Silhouette Books Newsletter absolutely free. *And Silhouette Romance is delivered free.*

Mail the coupon today to get your four free books—and more romance than you ever bargained for.

Silhouette Romance is a service mark and a registered trademark of Simon & Schuster, Inc.

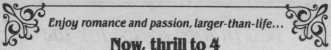

Enjoy romance and passion, larger-than-life...

Now, thrill to 4
Silhouette Intimate Moments
novels (a $9.00 value)—
ABSOLUTELY FREE!

If you want more passionate sensual romance, then Silhouette Intimate Moments novels are for you!

In every 256-page book, you'll find romance that's electrifying...involving... and intense. And now, these larger-than-life romances can come into your home every month!

4 FREE books as your introduction.

Act now and we'll send you four thrilling Silhouette Intimate Moments novels. They're our gift to introduce you to our convenient home subscription service. Every month, we'll send you four new Silhouette Intimate Moments books. Look them over for 15 days. If you keep them, pay just $9.00 for all four. Or return them at no charge.

We'll mail your books to you *as soon as they are published.* Plus, with every shipment, you'll receive the Silhouette Books Newsletter absolutely free. *And Silhouette Intimate Moments is delivered free.*

Mail the coupon today and start receiving Silhouette Intimate Moments. Romance novels for women...not girls.

Silhouette Intimate Moments

Silhouette Intimate Moments™
120 Brighton Road, P.O. Box 5020, Clifton, NJ 07015

☐ YES! Please send me FREE and without obligation, 4 exciting Silhouette Intimate Moments romance novels. Unless you hear from me after I receive my 4 FREE books, please send 4 new Silhouette Intimate Moments novels to preview each month. I understand that you will bill me $2.25 each for a total of $9.00 — with no additional shipping, handling or other charges. **There is no minimum number of books to buy and I may cancel anytime I wish.** The first 4 books are mine to keep, even if I never take a single additional book.

☐ Mrs. ☐ Miss ☐ Ms. ☐ Mr.   BMSK24

Name	(please print)

Address	Apt. #

City ( )	State	Zip

Area Code	Telephone Number

Signature (if under 18, parent or guardian must sign)

This offer, limited to one per household, expires May 31, 1985. Terms and prices are subject to change. Your enrollment is subject to acceptance by Simon & Schuster Enterprises.

Silhouette Intimate Moments is a service mark and trademark of Simon & Schuster, Inc.